THE
BROKEN HORSESHOE

Francis Durbridge

WILLIAMS & WHITING

Titles by Francis Durbridge to be published by Williams & Whiting

A Case For Paul Temple
A Game of Murder
A Man Called Harry Brent
A Time of Day
Bat Out of Hell
Breakaway – The Family Affair
Breakaway – The Local Affair
Death Comes to the Hibiscus (stage play – writing as Nicholas Vane)
La Boutique
Melissa
My Friend Charles
Paul Temple and the Alex Affair
Paul Temple and the Canterbury Case (film script)
Paul Temple and the Conrad Case
Paul Temple and the Curzon Case
Paul Temple and the Geneva Mystery
Paul Temple and the Gilbert Case
Paul Temple and the Gregory Affair
Paul Temple and the Jonathan Mystery
Paul Temple and the Lawrence Affair
Paul Temple and the Madison Mystery
Paul Temple and the Margo Mystery
Paul Temple and the Spencer Affair
Paul Temple and the Sullivan Mystery
Paul Temple and the Vandyke Affair
Paul Temple and Steve
Paul Temple Intervenes
Portrait of Alison
Send for Paul Temple (radio serial)
Send for Paul Temple (stage play)
Step In The Dark

The Broken Horseshoe
The Desperate People
The Doll
The Other Man
The Scarf
The Teckman Biography
The World of Tim Frazer
Three Plays for Radio Volume 1
Three Plays for Radio Volume 2
Tim Frazer and the Salinger Affair
Tim Frazer and the Mellin Forrest Mystery
Twenty Minutes From Rome
Two Paul Temple Plays for Radio
Two Paul Temple Plays for Television

Also by Francis Durbridge and published by Williams & Whiting:

Murder At The Weekend
Murder In The Media

Also published by Williams & Whiting:

Francis Durbridge : The Complete Guide
By Melvyn Barnes

This book reproduces Francis Durbridge's original script together with the list of characters and actors of the BBC programme on the dates mentioned, but the eventual broadcast might have edited Durbridge's script in respect of scenes, dialogue and character names.

INTRODUCTION

The Broken Horseshoe by Francis Durbridge was televised by the BBC in six thirty-minute episodes from 15 March to 19 April 1952. It was produced and directed by Martyn C. Webster, who had been Durbridge's consistent BBC radio producer since the 1930s - so this partnership, dating from the comparatively early days of radio, was likely to become a success when they turned to the growing medium of television. But what made *The Broken Horseshoe* so special, and so worthy of publishing the original script seventy years after it was transmitted?

Firstly, as an enthusiast and researcher of Francis Durbridge (1912-98), I can confirm that the BBC never repeated this serial and has never released it on DVD, for the simple reason that it was transmitted live from Alexandra Palace and recordings have therefore not been available. That gives this book the unique opportunity to bring to present day readers the original UK version of a television serial that enthralled viewers when BBC Television was still finding its way and developing its drama programming and reputation. My own researches in the BBC Written Archives, incidentally, revealed that Durbridge originally planned to call this serial *The Mark Fenton Story* - but it was under the rather more intriguing title of *The Broken Horseshoe* that it made history.

So why did *The Broken Horseshoe* have a significance that earned it a mention in reference books such as *The Hutchinson Chronology of World History?* The answer is straightforward, but firstly it might be useful to set this in the context of Francis Durbridge's career. By the time he turned his writing talents to television, he had already since 1933 been a prolific writer of sketches, stories, plays and serials for BBC radio, and had become arguably the most popular writer of mystery thrillers for radio. In 1938 he had found the niche in which he was to carve his name, when his radio serial *Send for Paul Temple* was a great success and his subsequent Paul Temple radio serials over several decades built an enormous UK and European fanbase. So it was natural that, while continuing to write for radio, he should join the rush of writers into the newer medium of television. Indeed this was much later confirmed in a published interview with Durbridge (*Radio Times*, 21 October 1971) when he said: "Twenty years ago in the United States, a producer told me that I was wasting my time by not going into television. So that's what I did – I tried to build up a reputation with serials, since I'd vowed never to write a Paul Temple episode for television."

The result was that in March 1952 *The Broken Horseshoe* became the first thriller serial on British television. There had already been one-off television plays in the mystery genre, two series (rather than serials) of Lester Powell's *The Inch Man* in 1951 and 1952, and even a 1951 series of Sherlock Holmes stories with Alan Wheatley as Holmes and Raymond Francis as Watson. But *The Broken Horseshoe* was a true UK television first, a thriller that was a genuine serial with one story continuing over several episodes, and that made it significant. Indeed it prompted C.A. Lejeune to review it in her *Observer* column (23 March 1952) in terms that now seem extraordinary. She wrote: "It will be interesting to see how Mr. Durbridge manages his 're-capping' from week to week, for *The Broken Horseshoe* is a true serial and not a series of associated adventures with a beginning, middle and end. The skill with which such a programme can arrange for new viewers to start viewing here, without boring old viewers or wasting time, will achieve much to do with the serial's success. But if it goes on as well as it has begun, I don't intend to miss a Saturday." From this it seems that Durbridge was at the time regarded as an innovator, although he had been doing that very thing for over ten years on the radio!

Very soon after, for Durbridge's second BBC Television serial *Operation Diplomat*, Martyn C. Webster was again the producer/director. But in Francis Durbridge's career on television *The Broken Horseshoe* was just the first step, and from that point he wrote for nearly thirty years a succession of brilliant and record-breaking television serials that attracted a huge body of viewers internationally – including *Portrait of Alison*, *My Friend Charles*, *The Other Man*, *The Scarf*, *The World of Tim Frazer*, *Melissa*, *Bat Out of Hell*, *The Passenger*, *The Doll* and *Breakaway*. And always he remained loyal to the BBC, in spite of blandishments from the new commercial television channel ITV.

Not surprisingly *The Broken Horseshoe* was very quickly turned into a cinema film, because four films based on Durbridge's Paul Temple radio serials had already proved popular. The 1953 Butchers/Nettlefold production of *The Broken Horseshoe* recruited Durbridge's radio/television producer Martyn C. Webster as director, but used A.R. Rawlinson rather than Durbridge to write the screenplay (although I would guess that Durbridge was involved). His next four television serials were also adapted for the cinema.

There are interesting points to be made about the casting of the film *The Broken Horseshoe*. Firstly, as film producers tended to cast popular actors from the cinema world rather than actors from television, John Robinson as Mark Fenton was replaced by cinema favourite Robert Beatty – and Beatty did it again in 1955, replacing television's Patrick Barr in the film version of Durbridge's *Portrait of Alison*. And secondly, there is the nice point that in the 1953 film of *The Broken Horseshoe* Inspector George Bellamy was played by Peter Coke, who assumed the mantle of Paul Temple on BBC radio in the following year and quickly became the public's definitive voice in this role.

So enjoy this script, the advent of Francis Durbridge on television.

Melvyn Barnes
Author of Francis Durbridge: The Complete Guide (Williams & Whiting 2018)

THE BROKEN HORSESHOE

A television serial in six parts

By FRANCIS DURBRIDGE

Broadcast live on BBC Television 15 March – 19 April 1952
Produced and Directed by Martyn C. Webster

CAST:

Mark Fenton	John Robinson
Duncan Craig	Andrew Crawford
Inspector George Bellamy	John Byron
Della Freeman	Barbara Lott
Charles Constance	Michael Yannis
Sister Rogers	Elizabeth Maude
Nurse Ann	Delphi Lawrence
The Postman	Fred Griffiths
Sergeant Lewis	John Baker
Railway Official	Frank Atkinson
A Waiter	Marc Sheldon
Felix Gallegos	Robert Adair
Jackie Leroy	Daphne Maddox
Sergeant West	Alec Ross
Superintendent Grayson	Tristan Rawson
Long	Russell Hunter
Ernest Carrel	John Witty
Walter Briggs	Noel Howlett
Police Clerk	Peter Fox
Keith Phipps	Arthur Ridley
Harry	Max Barrett
Hotel Receptionist	Marc Sheldon
The Barber	Alun Owen
Connie Haliday	Violet Oxley
Air stewardess	Jacqueline Lacey

Part One:

MR CONSTANCE

OPEN TO: The main entrance of a large London Hospital. Nurses, Doctors, students, etc passing to and fro.

CUT TO: A plaque reading "St Matthew's Hospital"

CUT TO: Corridor of hospital.
The SISTER and NURSE ANN pass FENTON and nod, but FENTON ignores them. FENTON walks up to a door and opens it wide. We see GEORGE BELLAMY at a desk. The door closes. Camera tracks up to read "PRIVATE" and there is a small card, in a holder, which reads: "MR MARK FENTON".

FENTON is in his late thirties. He is wearing part of a dark suit and a white surgeon's jacket. He looks worried. FENTON enters his room and closes the door behind him. The room is furnished as a study, books, house-phone, telephone, cigarette box, desk diary, medical magazines, etc, on the desk.

GEORGE is sitting in an armchair watching FENTON. GEORGE is about fifty-two or three. He wears a trench style raincoat; a trilby hat is resting on his knee.

FENTON looks at GEORGE but makes no sign of recognition. He takes out a bunch of keys and locks the door. Having done this, he crosses to the desk, takes a cigarette from the box, and then sits in the swivel chair behind the desk and is facing GEORGE.

FENTON lights his cigarette and watches GEORGE, his expression betraying neither interest nor curiosity. He sits smoking, his eyes on the visitor. After a moment he leans forward, picks up the telephone receiver, puts it down on the desk, and knocks down the switch on the House-phone.

3

FENTON: Now we shan't be disturbed. How long have you been here, George?

GEORGE: (*Glancing at his watch*) About forty minutes. You said three o'clock.

FENTON: Yes, I'm sorry. I thought I should be finished by three. (*A moment*) How's Jane?

GEORGE: She's very well. A little worried, of course.

FENTON: About me?

GEORGE: Naturally.

FENTON: Tell her not to worry. Everything's going to be all right.

GEORGE: I hope so, Mark.

FENTON: (*Serious*) Is this an official visit, George – or off the record?

GEORGE: Official, of course. Just because you happen to be my brother-in-law you mustn't expect preferential treatment.

FENTON: But I do! What's the point of having a brother-in-law at Scotland Yard if you can't pull a few strings for me. And talking of preferential treatment, why is it you're an Inspector? You've only been at the Yard for six years. I know a man who's been a full-blown Sergeant for twelve.

GEORGE: Perhaps he never solved a murder.

FENTON: Ah, yes, you solved a murder once, didn't you, George? I hadn't thought of that.

GEORGE: Mark, I told Jane I was coming this afternoon. She said she'd like to see you. Why don't you drop in on Sunday? Come to lunch if you feel like it.

FENTON: (*Obviously tired*) Thanks, but I've had rather a busy week. I'll see what happens. (*Looks up*) I've prepared this statement. (*Takes document from desk*) Don't worry, I typed it myself. (*Hands it to

4

GEORGE) Read it. If you think it'll satisfy the Yard, I'll sign it.

(*GEORGE looks at the document in his hand*)

FENTON: Go on, read it …

GEORGE: Does it satisfy you?

FENTON: What do you mean?

GEORGE: Your conscience. You've told me three versions already.

FENTON: My conscience is clear. It always has been.

(*GEORGE looks very serious*)

GEORGE: Look, I don't think you realise just how serious this business is. This is murder. You're in a spot. A much worse spot than you imagine.

FENTON: What do you mean?

GEORGE: (*Watching FENTON's reactions*) If I were you I should let a good lawyer see this before you give it to me officially.

FENTON: Wait. Let me tell you the whole thing. Not just what happened to me, but the complete story up to date.

GEORGE: Do you know the complete story, Mark?

FENTON: (*Nodding at the manuscript in George's hand*) I've fitted the pieces together. What you told me, what Della told me and what I found out for myself. It started five weeks ago, on February 8th to be precise. February 8th … I think it was a Friday … Yes, Friday … I was on call that night and I arrived at the hospital at about a quarter to ten …

CUT TO: Exterior shot of a large modern Ambulance racing along the Brompton Road. "Accident" sign flicking on and off.

FENTON's VOICE: … Just before midnight a man was knocked down on the Brompton Road. He was

5

brought to the hospital. His name was Charles Constance.

CUT TO: *A nurse pushing a trolley of surgical instruments, bandages, etc, down the corridor.*

CUT TO: Surgical instruments being sterilised in a steel container.

CUT TO: *A patient being wheeled on a rolling-stretcher towards an operating theatre. Track in tight to the patient (CHARLES CONSTANCE) being wheeled through the swing-doors of the operating room.*

CUT TO: *NURSE ANN is assisting SISTER ROGERS to adjust her surgical mask. FENTON and several nurses are in the operating theatre.*

CUT TO: Interior FENTON's room. Night.
SISTER ROGERS is sitting at the desk writing a report. DR CRAIG enters. He is a good-looking young Scotsman.
SISTER: (*Looking up*) Hello, Doctor!
CRAIG: Hello, Sister! I thought you were off duty tonight.
SISTER: (*Smiling*) I am.
CRAIG: My, but you're a glutton for work! How is that accident case?
(*CRAIG sits in the armchair and sucks his pipe*)
SISTER: Well, he's back in the ward now and that's as much as one can say. How's your case?
CRAIG: Mr Armitage? Don't mention Mr Armitage, Sister, please! I'm going to get that man better just for the cheer joy of being able to kick his posterior.   Do you know what he was doing just now when I walked into the ward?

6

SISTER: No?

CRAIG: Smoking a cigar!

SISTER: A cigar!

CRAIG: A cigar! Heaven knows where he gets them from! I think they must be smuggled into him by the night nurse.

SISTER: Dr Craig, I'll have you know that Sister Evans is thoroughly reliable, and if you're going to suggest …

CRAIG: (*Interrupting, laughing*) I know, I know! I'm only pulling your leg!

SISTER: You Scots and your sense of humour!

(*FENTON enters*)

CRAIG: How did it go?

FENTON: (*With a slight shrug*) Not too well, I'm afraid. Nasty concussion with a depressed fracture.

CRAIG: (*Non-committal*) M'm. Who is he, do you know?

FENTON: (*Looking towards SISTER; casually*) I don't know. Rather a curious looking chap. A foreigner I should imagine.

(*SISTER looks at a card which she has taken from the desk*)

SISTER: His name's Constance. He's staying at a hotel in Southampton Row.

CRAIG: What happened, exactly?

FENTON: He was knocked down by a car …

SISTER: Yes, and the driver didn't even have the decency to stop.

(*FENTON looks at the SISTER*)

FENTON: (*Curious*) How do you know?

SISTER: The police rang through about a quarter of an hour ago. They wanted a report on him. I told them you were operating.

FENTON: Oh.

7

CRAIG: (*Rising from the armchair*) Good Lord, can you imagine anybody not stopping after running someone down?

FENTON: Was it the police who identified him?

SISTER: No, this card was found in one of his pockets. It seems to be the only means of identification.

(*FENTON takes the card from the SISTER. It is a hotel registration card with certain details – underlined – being in handwriting.*

It reads:

HOTEL SEATON
Southampton Row
London, W.C.1.
Name: Mr Constance
Date: Feb 7th '52
Room: 108
Price: 27/6, room only.

(Telephone rings)

SISTER: Excuse me. (*Lifts receiver on desk*)

CUT TO: Exterior Telephone Booth in a deserted London square.

CUT TO: Interior telephone booth. Night.

DELLA: (*After a moment*) Hello? This is the Hotel Seaton, Southampton Row. I'm sorry to disturb you, but we're rather anxious to get some news about a Mr Constance. Yes, yes, that's right … We heard about the accident … An operation? … When? … Oh, I see … Oh, yes, he frequently stays here – he's   an old friend of ours … No, he's from Birmingham … Wait a moment and I'll give you the address ... (*She puts her hand over the receiver, waits a moment, then:*) ... The address he gave us was The Kings Hotel, New Street ... Yes ... Well, I do hope he'll be all right ... Yes, I'm sure you will ... Thank you. (*She replaces the receiver*)

CUT TO: *FENTON and CRAIG are standing by CHARLES CONSTANCE's bed in earnest consultation. Hypodermic syringe, small medicine jars and bottles etc are on the table by the bed. CRAIG takes the hypodermic syringe, opens one of the small jars, and prepares the injection.*

FENTON'S VOICE: (*Over action*) Things looked very bad for Charles Constance, we thought he wouldn't recover. About four o'clock on the following afternoon, Saturday, February 9th, I had a consultation with Dr Craig, and we decided to give him a Nikethamide injection. It was our last chance of saving him.

CUT TO: Interior of FENTON's room. Day.

SISTER is sitting at Dr Fenton's desk. She is holding a fountain pen in a bottle of ink and is filling it; then she continues writing a letter. FENTON enters; he turns and speaks to CRAIG who is standing in the corridor behind him.

FENTON: I think we'd both better take a look at him this evening, Craig. I'll give you a ring just before six.

CRAIG: Yes, all right, old man. Don't leave it any later or I shall go with Armitage. By George, I'd like to give him an injection!

(*FENTON laughs and closes the door behind him.*)

SISTER: Oh dear, I always seem to be using your desk. I hope you don't mind.

FENTON: Of course not. No, don't get up.

9

SISTER: This is about the only place in the building where I'm not disturbed. How's the patient?

FENTON: Constance?

SISTER: Yes.

FENTON: Not too good, I'm afraid. Dr Craig's just given him some Nikethamide – intravenously.

SISTER: It's as bad as that?

FENTON: I'm afraid so. (*Knock on the door*) Come in!

(*FENTON opens the door. GEORGE, his brother-in-law, is standing in the doorway. He wears a dark overcoat and carries a bowler hat*)

FENTON: Why, hello, George! Come in! Do you know Sister: my brother-in-law, Sister. Inspector Bellamy.

SISTER: How do you do, Inspector?

FENTON: Sit down.

GEORGE: I think we spoke on the phone, Sister – this morning.

(*SISTER looks puzzled*)

GEORGE: About Mr Constance.

SISTER: Oh, yes, of course!

GEORGE: (*To Fenton*) How is he?

FENTON: We were just talking about him. His condition's serious.

GEORGE: Is he conscious?

FENTON: No.

GEORGE: M'm. (*Turning towards the SISTER*) Have you got that card you mentioned?

SISTER: The hotel registration?

GEORGE: Yes.

FENTON: It's in the left-hand drawer.

(*SISTER opens the drawer and finds the card.*)

FENTON: George, why are you so interested in this man? Is he a crook or something?

GEORGE: We don't know who he is – or what he is. We're interested in him because he was deliberately knocked down by an unknown gentleman in a Rolls.

FENTON: When you say – deliberately – you mean the car didn't stop?

GEORGE: I mean what I say, Mark. The man in the Rolls was waiting for him. Constance was quite deliberately run down. (*Takes card from Sister*) Thank you, Sister. (*Looks at the card*) Hotel Seaton, Southampton Row ... M'm ... (*Looks up*) I don't suppose I should tell you this, but – there isn't an Hotel Seaton, at least not in Southampton Row.

SISTER: But the hotel telephoned!

GEORGE: (*Shaking his head*) We've checked the call. It's a call-box in Russell Square.

(*SISTER stares at FENTON in amazement*)

SISTER: And what about the card?

GEORGE: It's a fake.

FENTON: You mean it was printed specially for Mr Constance?

GEORGE: Whether it was printed specially for Constance or not we don't know, that's one of the questions we want to ask him.

FENTON: Well, I doubt whether you ever will.

SISTER: (*To GEORGE; puzzled*) A call-box in Russell Square?

GEORGE: (*Nodding*) Yes. Sister, what was it the girl said to you on the phone?

SISTER: I told you this morning. She said that Mr Constance was a friend of theirs. She gave me an address in Birmingham. I think she said the King's Hotel, New Street.

GEORGE: Yes, that's right. (*Smiling*) That's what you said this morning.

FENTON: You won't catch Sister. She's got an excellent memory.

SISTER: Yes, indeed I have, and I've remembered I should be in the ward where I'll be if you want me to answer any more questions.

(*SISTER leaves*)

FENTON: Did you check the address in Birmingham?

GEORGE: We did.

FENTON: Don't tell me: there isn't a King's Hotel.

GEORGE: Oh, there's a King's Hotel all right, but they've never heard of Mr Constance.

FENTON: (*Amused*) No, I'll bet they haven't! Do you know what I think? I think Constance was probably running away from a girlfriend and this chap in the Rolls was the girl's father.

GEORGE: Why, that's brilliant, Mark! And the hotel card – and the girl in the telephone box?

FENTON: (*Laughing*) That's your pigeon, thank goodness!

(*They cross to the door*)

GEORGE: Do you think I will be able to talk to Constance?

FENTON: I don't know. I'll let you know. Did you play golf at the weekend?

GEORGE: I did. (*On his favourite subject*) You know that absolute stinker – the fourth – the dog leg?

FENTON: Yes.

GEORGE: I did it in three.

FENTON: Really! I don't know how you do it, George.

GEORGE: I concentrate, old boy – and keep my eye on the ball.

FENTON: I keep my eye on the ball! (*Amused*) I never hit it far enough to do anything else.

(*They laugh. FENTON opens the door. DELLA comes in and closes the door. She is carrying a small bunch of flowers*)

DELLA: Excuse me, doctor. Could you spare me a moment?

FENTON: (*Hesitating*) Well ...

DELLA: (*A shade nervous*) I did try to make an appointment, but they said that you couldn't see me before Thursday and I did want to see you before, because, well, I ... (*She smiles at him*) I shan't keep you a moment. Thank you.

FENTON: You'd better come in.

DELLA: Thank you.

GEORGE: (*Amused*) I'll phone you tomorrow, Mark. Let me know if there's any change in his condition.

FENTON: (*To GEORGE; but looking at DELLA*) Yes, of course.

(*GEORGE smiles and leaves*)

FENTON: Sit down. I expect the Sister told you that I only see visitors by appointment.

DELLA: (*Turning*) Yes, she did. But you see, ... I just wanted to ask you something, that's all.

FENTON: (*Facing her*) Well? (*Smiling*) Go on.

DELLA: Do you perform all the operations here – in this hospital I mean?

FENTON: (*Amused*) Well, not all of them – but I manage to get my share.

DELLA: But you operated on Charles Constance?

FENTON: Yes, as matter of fact I did. He was brought here on Friday night, when I happened to be on call.

DELLA: (*Hesitant*) Was your operation successful?

FENTON: (*Watching her*) Is Mr Constance a friend of yours?

DELLA: (*Hesitating*) Yes.

FENTON: A close friend?

DELLA: He's a friend of mine.

13

FENTON: Is that why you wanted to see me, just to inquire about Mr Constance?

DELLA: Yes.

FENTON: But you could have inquired at the desk. (*Smiling*) That's the usual procedure, you know.

DELLA: Yes, I know it is, but – I wanted to know the truth. Is he going to get better?

FENTON: (*After a moment*) Is he your husband?

DELLA: No.

FENTON: Are you a relative?

DELLA: I've told you. I'm just a friend.

FENTON: I see. (*Studying her closely*) You know, Miss – er?

DELLA: Freeman.

FENTON: You know Miss Freeman, you're not the only one interested in Mr Constance. (*Watching her; obviously intrigued*) The police seem to think that the accident wasn't exactly an accident.

DELLA: (*Relieved*) Oh, I see. You still haven't answered my question, doctor.

FENTON: I don't know whether he's going to get better or not. I wouldn't like to say. The operation was more difficult than we expected.

DELLA: Is he conscious?

FENTON: No.

DELLA: Well, may I leave these flowers for him?

FENTON: Yes, of course. (*He takes the flowers and puts them down on the desk.*)

DELLA: He'll know who they're from.

FENTON: And your address, in case he should want to get in touch with you?

DELLA: I'm staying at the Park Lane Hotel. I shall be there until March 3rd. But I'll phone you tomorrow morning, about nine o'clock, if I may.

14

FENTON: Yes, all right. Ask for extension 79. (*Smiling*) My name is Fenton, by the way. Dr Mark Fenton. You've got to stress the Mark because we've got another Fenton here and it's rather confusing.

DELLA: Thank you, doctor. You've been very kind.

FENTON: Not at all. (*He opens the door*) I'm sorry I haven't better news for you. (*They shake hands*) Good-bye.

DELLA: Good-bye. (*She goes out*)

(*FENTON closes the door and returns to the desk. He looks thoughtful; stares down at the flowers. Suddenly he notices a visiting card tucked away amongst them. He picks up and stares at the card; puzzled. There is a rough sketch on the card of a Broken Horseshoe. FENTON gazes into space for a few seconds. He lifts the flowers and smells them*)

FENTON's VOICE: (*Over action*) It's strange how certain people make an impression on you, isn't it, George? I couldn't forget Della Freeman. For the rest of that afternoon, I found myself thinking about her. I wanted to ask Constance a hundred and one questions about this friend of his, who she was, where she came from, and what the little drawing meant on the card with the flowers. But I must tell you about Charles Constance. On Monday evening, three days after the operation, a miracle happened. Constance regained consciousness and asked for a cigarette.

CUT TO: *CONSTANCE is a thin, dark, sallow looking man. NURSE ANN is standing by his bed taking his temperature. The Nurse takes the thermometer out of his mouth, smiles at him, and marks the temperature chart she is holding. CONSTANCE closes his eyes. FENTON crosses over to the bed.*

15

FENTON:	(*To Nurse*) Well? How's your patient, Nurse?
NURSE:	He seems very much better.
FENTON:	(*He feels CONSTANCE's pulse*) M'm – not bad. (*He looks at CONSTANCE*) Temperature?

(*NURSE hands FENTON the chart*)

FENTON:	M'm. I see. Has Dr Craig seen him?
NURSE:	Not yet. Dr Gillespie saw him this afternoon. He seemed very pleased.
FENTON:	(*Nodding*) I want you to continue the hourly pulse and temperature chart. Notify sister if his pulse changes.
NURSE:	Yes, sir.

(*FENTON looks down at CONSTANCE who moves and opens his eyes.*)

FENTON:	Well – how are you feeling?
CONSTANCE:	(*With an attractive foreign accent*) I'd … like … a cigarette …

(*NURSE smiles*)

FENTON:	Yes, I expect you would, but – I'm sorry. Does your head hurt you?
CONSTANCE:	No, I just feel … very thirsty, that's all …
FENTON:	Would you like a drink of water?

(*CONSTANCE nods and NURSE gets the glass from the table.*)

CONSTANCE:	(*Sipping the water*) Which hospital is this?
FENTON:	It's St Matthew's, in Kensington. Now don't worry, and don't try to talk, just relax.
CONSTANCE:	What day is it?
FENTON:	It's Monday.
CONSTANCE:	How long have I been here?

16

FENTON: Since Friday night. You had an accident.
               You were knocked down by a car. There's
               nothing for you to worry about.
CONSTANCE: I remember the car … (*Weakly*) A large
               car, it … was … going … very …fast …
               (*He closes his eyes*)
(*FENTON feels his pulse again. He nods to the NURSE*)
FENTON: I'll get Dr Craig to see him first thing
               tomorrow morning. Will you be on duty?
NURSE: Yes, sir.
FENTON: Don't forget the hourly pulse chart.
(*FENTON stands looking down at CONSTANCE*)

FENTON's VOICE: (*Over action*) I was on leave from the
                  hospital for two days, but when I returned,
                  on the Thursday morning, I noticed a
                  considerable improvement in Constance.
                  There was no longer any doubt. He was
                  going to get better.

CUT TO: *The NURSE enters the ward and crosses to
CONSTANCE. He is in bed with a thermometer in his mouth.
The flowers are in a vase on the table by the bed. FENTON
comes into shot and stands looking down at CONSTANCE.
The NURSE takes the thermometer out of his mouth, marks
the temperature chart, and moves out of shot.*
FENTON: Well, how are you feeling this morning?
CONSTANCE: Very much better.
FENTON: You certainly look better. Does your leg
               hurt at all?
CONSTANCE: Slightly, when I move it. Are you Mr
               Fenton?
FENTON: Yes.

CONSTANCE: The Matron told me that you operated on me. I want to thank you.

FENTON: You've been a very good patient.

CONSTANCE: And a very lucky one – to have found such a good doctor. (*With a smile*) By the way, there seems to have been a certain amount of curiosity about my identity.

FENTON: Identity?

CONSTANCE: Yes. A detective came here last night – he asked me a lot of questions.

FENTON: Well, I expect that's because you were knocked down and the car didn't stop.

CONSTANCE: Yes, I expect so. But he asked me about a hotel in – what did he say – Southampton Row? The Hotel Seaton. I've never heard of it.

FENTON: You were not staying there?

CONSTANCE: But of course not. I live in London. (*Smiling*) My name is Charles Constance. I am thirty-nine years of age, I am a bachelor, a musician, and I have a small service flat in Earl's Court. I also smoke – incessantly – when permitted.

FENTON: Well, I'm afraid you're not permitted, Mr Constance – not at the moment. Tell me, do you remember anything about the accident?

CONSTANCE: I saw the car coming towards me; it was going very fast. That's all I remember. (*Changing the subject*) How long do you think it will be, before I am able to leave?

FENTON: A fortnight – perhaps three weeks. It's early days yet.

CONSTANCE: I'll bet you twenty pounds I shall be out of here in ten days.

18

FENTON:	We shall see. (*A shade too casual*) By the way, I notice you've got your flowers.
CONSTANCE:	Yes. Thank you very much.
FENTON:	Don't thank me, thank Miss Freeman. Incidentally, she sent you a card. (*Examining the flowers*) It should be here somewhere. (*Picks up the card*)
CONSTANCE:	(*Puzzled*) But I thought the flowers were from the hospital – all part of the National Health.
FENTON:	Oh, no! Your friend Miss Freeman sent them. As a matter of fact, she delivered them herself. Here's the card.

(*CONSTANCE takes the card from FENTON. He stares at it bewildered*)

FENTON:	Well?
CONSTANCE:	A broken horseshoe? What does that mean?
FENTON:	(*Smiling*) I'm afraid I don't know. Miss Freeman's your friend, not mine. I was rather hoping you'd explain the joke to me.
CONSTANCE:	(*Puzzled*) But I don't understand. (*With a laugh*) I think perhaps the Sister must have made a mistake and delivered the flowers to the wrong patient.
FENTON:	(*Shaking his head*) The Sister had nothing to do with it; the flowers were given to me.
CONSTANCE:	(*Amused*) But I don't know anyone called Freeman! And why should a complete stranger send me flowers? This is most amusing! Tell me, what was she like, this girl?

19

FENTON: She was dark, fairly tall, good looking, she'd got very nice eyes … Look here, you must know her! Why she telephoned on Tuesday morning to see how you were getting along.

CONSTANCE: (*Shaking his head*) I can assure you, I've never set eyes on the young lady. I don't even know anyone called Freeman!

(*FENTON looks puzzled*)

CONSTANCE: Was she English?

FENTON: Why, yes – at least – I should imagine so.

CONSTANCE: (*Watching FENTON; faintly amused*) And attractive?

FENTON: (*Just a shade irritated*) Yes, I've told you, she was – very attractive.

CONSTANCE: I just can't imagine who it could be. (*With an emphatic shrug*) I just can't imagine. (*He looks at FENTON and smiles*) I'm sorry, doctor. (*Stares down at the card he is holding; the card from Della*)

CUT TO: The card showing the picture of a Broken Horseshoe.

CUT TO: Interior of FENTON's Room. Day.
CRAIG is at the desk writing a report.

FENTON's VOICE: (*Over action*) Mr Constance would have won his bet. He left the hospital on Wednesday, February 27th. Needless to say he wasn't really fit, but he was anxious to leave, and – well, anyhow, he came to see me the morning he was leaving. Dr Craig was in my office.

20

(*There is a knock on the door. CRAIG looks up and blots the paper he has been writing on.*)

CRAIG: Come in!

(*CONSTANCE enters; he is smoking and walks with the aid of a stick. The stick is an unusual one and has a very ornate head.*)

CONSTANCE: Oh, I beg your pardon. I wanted to see Dr Fenton.

CRAIG: (*Rising*) He'll be here in a minute. Sit down. Over here – it's a bit more comfortable.

(*CONSTANCE sits in the armchair*)

CRAIG: I understand you're leaving us this morning?

CONSTANCE: Yes.

CRAIG: How do you feel?

CONSTANCE: Not too bad.

CRAIG: And not too good, eh?

CONSTANCE: I shall be all right. I'll take things easy for a little while.

CRAIG: And so you ought. I should get out of the city. Go down to the sea for a few days. Get some fresh air in your lungs.

CONSTANCE: I may go up to Scotland. I've got some friends in Dundee.

CRAIG: Dundee. Couldn't be better! Wish I was coming with you.

(*FENTON enters*)

FENTON: Hello, Constance! (*To CRAIG*) Craig, have you seen my cigarette lighter?

CRAIG: No. (*Looks at desk*) It wasn't on the desk.

FENTON: I've been looking all over the place for it. I must have left it at the flat.

CRAIG: I've finished the Stimpson report.

FENTON: Good. I've just had a look at Armitage.
               His blood sugar levels are low.

CRAIG: What again? I gave him an infusion this
               morning.

FENTON: He needs another.

CRAIG: Ye Gods, I suppose he does. (*To
               CONSTANCE: crossing towards the door*)
               Give my regards to civilisation. (*He goes
               out*)

FENTON: What does he mean?

CONSTANCE: I told him I may be going up to Scotland.

FENTON: Oh, I see. (*He looks at CONSTANCE*)
               Well – how's the leg?

CONSTANCE: Oh, it's all right.

FENTON: (*Shaking his head*) It's not all right, you
               shouldn't be leaving yet – but I suppose
               you know that.

CONSTANCE: Yes, I know – but – (*Smiles*) I'm leaving
               just the same.

FENTON: (*Opens his diary on the desk*) Well, I think
               you'd better come and see me at the end of
               next week, just for a check over.

CONSTANCE: Yes, all right, doctor.

FENTON: Thursday, March 6th, ten o'clock.
               (*Scribbles in his diary*) Just let me see you
               walk to the door. No, don't use the stick.

CONSTANCE: (*Walks to the door*) And thank you again,
               you've been very kind.

FENTON: By the way, I happened to tell my brother-
               in-law about that girl – Miss Freeman. He
               was most interested.

CONSTANCE: Your brother-in-law?

FENTON: Yes. He's the chap who asked you all those questions. You remember, from Scotland Yard.

CONSTANCE: Oh! (*Amused*) I didn't realise he was your brother-in-law.

FENTON: (*Nodding*) He was rather interested in Miss Freeman, so much so in fact that he checked up on her. (*Watching CONSTANCE's reaction*) She was staying at the Park Lane Hotel.

CONSTANCE: Oh. (*Hesitant*) Did he see her?

FENTON: No, apparently, she left the hotel on the nineteenth.

(*CONSTANCE looks relieved*)

FENTON: Are you sure she wasn't a friend of yours, Mr Constance?

CONSTANCE: Quite sure.

FENTON: (*Nodding, holding out his hand*) Well, goodbye – and good luck.

CONSTANCE: Thank you.

(*CONSTANCE shakes hand with FENTON and then turns towards the door. He suddenly hesitates*)

CONSTANCE: Oh, Dr Fenton, I wonder if I could ask you a favour?

FENTON: Well – what is it?

(*CONSTANCE returns to the desk; takes an envelope from his pocket*)

CONSTANCE: Do you think I could leave this letter with you – well, until I see you at the end of next week? (*Holds out the envelope*)

FENTON: (*Takes letter*) Yes, I suppose so if you want to.

CONSTANCE: You see, it's addressed to a friend of mine,
              and I don't want to post it, not if
              everything's going to be all right.
FENTON: What do you mean, if everything's going
              to be all right? (*He leans back in his chair;
              studies CONSTANCE*)   Look   here,
              Constance, I don't want you to leave this
              hospital with any illusions about yourself,
              on the other hand I don't want you to get
              the wrong impression. You're not fit, but
              if you can take it easy for six months,
              you'll be as well as you've ever been.
              Probably better.
CONSTANCE: (*Smiling*) I would still like to leave the
              letter with you, Mr Fenton.
FENTON: Leave the letter by all means, you can pick
              it up at the end of next week.

(*FENTON opens a drawer in the desk and drops the letter
inside.*)

CONSTANCE: Perhaps I can do you a favour, doctor?
FENTON: Yes?
CONSTANCE: Would you like to make some easy
              money?
FENTON: Of course! Who wouldn't!
CONSTANCE: There's a horse running at Hurst Park, on
              Friday week – Siesta. Believe me, it's a
              certainty. It can't lose.
FENTON: (*Laughing*) It won't be a certainty if I back
              it!
CONSTANCE: Well, don't forget I told you. (*Crosses to
              the door*) If I don't see you, perhaps you'll
              be kind enough to post the letter for me. I
              have stamped it.

FENTON: Yes, all right. (*Smiling*) But I shall expect
                    to see you. In fact, I insist on it.
                    Thursday, March 6th, ten o'clock …
CONSTANCE: (*Amused; opening the door*) All right,
                    doctor. And again, many thanks …
(*CONSTANCE goes. FENTON opens his diary and picks up a
pen from the desk. There is a "buzz" on the dictograph.*)
FENTON: (*Switching the key down; speaking into
                    dictograph*) Yes?
CRAIG's VOICE: (*Exasperated*) Fenton, this is Craig, for
                    goodness sake come up and give me a
                    hand with Armitage. I'm having an awful
                    time.
FENTON: (*Amused*) I'll be right up.
(*FENTON closes his diary and rises.*)

CUT TO: A street near the hospital, late afternoon. Pillar
box in the foreground.

FENTON's VOICE: (*Over action*) Constance didn't turn up
                    at the hospital on the Thursday so on
                    Friday afternoon, March 7th, I took his
                    letter down to the pillar box. It was
                    addressed to Mrs Kelsey, at 27 Drayton
                    Court.
(*A POSTMAN rides up to the pillar box on his bicycle. He
dismounts, props the bicycle against the kerb, unlocks the box
and proceeds to empty the contents of the box into the sack he
is carrying. He is whistling to himself.*)
FENTON's VOICE: (*Over action*) On the way down to the
                    pillar box I started thinking about Della
                    Freeman. I wondered if Constance had lied
                    to me and if, by any chance, Mrs Kelsey

25

and Della were one and the same person
…

(*FENTON comes into shot. He is wearing a dark overcoat, a homburg hat, and gloves. Carries several letters. He stops by the pillar box.*)

FENTON:	Good evening.
POSTMAN:	Good evening, doctor.
FENTON:	Am I too late?
POSTMAN:	No, that's all right, you can drop them in here. (*Opens the sack in front of FENTON*)
FENTON:	Thank you. (*Drops all the letters into the sack except the one from CONSTANCE*)
POSTMAN:	You're not supposed to drop them in 'ere, you know – by rights you should pop 'em in the box.
FENTON:	Oh, I didn't know that.
POSTMAN:	Yes, regulations. Usual red-tape …
FENTON:	How's the wife?
POSTMAN:	Oh, very much better, doctor. There's been a great improvement this last week.
FENTON:	Splendid.
POSTMAN:	She's been better tempered too, thank Heavens. (*Chuckling*) She'll be better still, tonight.
FENTON:	Why tonight, particularly?
POSTMAN:	(*Grinning*) I backed a beauty this afternoon – it fairly romped home. Siesta. Twelve an' a 'alf to one.
FENTON:	(*Curious*) Siesta? Was that at Hurst Park?
POSTMAN:	Yes.
FENTON:	(*Thoughtfully*) That's funny, do you know I had that tip over a week ago.
POSTMAN:	Did you do it?

26

FENTON: (*His thoughts elsewhere*) No.
POSTMAN: (*Laughing*) Bad luck, doc! (*Points to the letter in FENTON's hand*) Are you going to post that?
FENTON: M'm? (*Suddenly realises that the letter is in his hand.*) Oh, er – where is Drayton Court, do you er – know?
POSTMAN: Yes, it's just off the Cromwell Road – near Victoria and Albert. About five minutes' walk from here.
FENTON: Oh. (*Suddenly*) I think I'll deliver this one.
POSTMAN: O.K. (*Crosses to his bicycle*)
FENTON: Give my regards to your wife.
POSTMAN: Thank you, doctor.

(*The POSTMAN gets on his bicycle and, with a nod to FENTON, rides away*)

FENTON's VOICE: (*Over action*) Drayton Court was a large, modern block of flats near Hyde Park Gate. Number 27 was on the third floor.

CUT TO: Shot of Drayton Court.

CUT TO: Interior Drayton Court. Day.

The lift door opens and Fenton gets out of it. He goes to the door of Number 27, presses the bell push and waits.

FENTON's VOICE: (*Over action*) I rang the bell but received no reply.

(*There is the sound of music from inside the flat*)

FENTON's VOICE: I waited a little while and then rang the bell again.

(*FENTON rings the bell again*)

FENTON's VOICE: I couldn't understand why no one answered the door because I could hear a radio playing inside the flat. Suddenly, I realised that the door was unlatched.

(*A cat pushes its way through the opening of the door and rushes out of the flat. FENTON pushes the door open with his foot and looks inside*)

FENTON's VOICE: I pushed the door open and looked inside …

(*FENTON enters the hall of the flat. It is a small hall; the door to the drawing room is open. He crosses and looks into the drawing room. The room is a shambles; desk ransacked; drawers hanging out of cupboards; cushions scattered across the settee; nest of tables overturned, etc. The radio continues to play; it is on the floor by the side of an overturned table. The body of CHARLES CONSTANCE is lying face downwards on the hearth in front of the fireplace.*)

FENTON's VOICE: I couldn't see his face, but I knew instinctively that it was Charles Constance. And I knew that he was dead. He'd been strangled.

(*FENTON crosses to CONSTANCE, kneels down, and makes a very brief examination of the body. He does not remove his gloves. He rises. Looks round the room, taking stock of the situation; bewildered and confused. Takes the letter from his pocket and stares at it*)

FENTON's VOICE: It was obvious that someone – perhaps the murderer – had been searching for something and I wondered if, by any chance, that something was in the letter which Constance had asked me to post to Mrs Kelsey. I opened the letter.

(*FENTON opens the envelope, extracts a small white ticket and examines it*)

FENTON's VOICE: There was a ticket inside – nothing else just a ticket. A first class, single, railway ticket from London, Paddington, to Birmingham, Snow Hill. The date on the ticket was February 24th. I

28

put the ticket in my pocket and looked round for the telephone.

(FENTON puts the envelope and the ticket in his pocket; looks round for the telephone)

FENTON's VOICE: I wanted to ring you, George. I knew that, at all cost, I must get in touch with Scotland Yard. (*Slowly*) It was while I was looking for the telephone … that … I … saw … the … mirror … It was on the wall, opposite the fireplace …

(The oval peach-glass mirror has scrawled across it in lipstick a copy of the sketch on Della's card – the Broken Horseshoe. FENTON, grave and mystified, stares at the Broken Horseshoe)

END OF PART ONE

Part Two:

MR FELIX GALLEGOS

OPEN TO: *FENTON stands in the drawing room of 27 Drayton Court. We see his reflection in the mirror with the Broken Horseshoe scrawled on it with lipstick.*

FENTON's VOICE: (*Over action*) It was while I was looking for the phone … that … I … saw … the … mirror … It was on the wall, opposite the fireplace …

(*FENTON switches off the radio. He turns away, looking for the telephone. He notices it on the desk. The base of the instrument has been unscrewed and the inside partly torn away*)

CUT TO: Telephone box on the corner of a street near Drayton Court.

CUT TO: Interior. Telephone Box. Day.
(*FENTON presses Button A*)
FENTON: Hello? Will you put me through to Inspector Bellamy, please? … Thank you … (*A pause*) George? This is Mark. Listen – I'm speaking from a callbox near Drayton Court. I want you to come here straight away – it's urgent. (*A moment*) It's Mr Constance – he's been murdered. Yes … strangled ... 27, Drayton Court – it's in Vernier Street, just off the Cromwell Road ... No, I haven't touched anything ... I'll tell you when I see you ... Yes, all right.

(*He replaces receiver*)

CUT TO: *FENTON walking towards Drayton Court. A taxi stops opposite the main entrance. DELLA FREEMAN gets out. FENTON starts running.*

33

FENTON's VOICE: You told me to go back to Drayton Court
and wait for you at the flat. I noticed a car had
stopped outside the block and Della Freeman got
out. As soon as I saw her, I knew instinctively
that she was on her way to Number 27.

CUT TO: Interior. The Entrance Hall of Drayton Court is
small, carpeted, as in luxury block of flats.
DELLA is standing by the lift door, her hand on the bell push.
FENTON: (*Calling; out of shot*) Miss Freeman!!!
(*DELLA turns. FENTON comes in, slightly out of breath
through running*)
DELLA: Why, hello!
(*She is completely at ease; pleasant manner*)
FENTON: I wasn't sure at first, but – I thought it was you.
DELLA: This is a surprise, Mr Fenton! Do you live here?
FENTON: No … (*He is still out of breath*) I've just been
down to the phone box on the corner. (*Seriously*)
What are you doing here?
DELLA: I asked you that question. (*Smiling*)
FENTON: I came to see a Mrs Kelsey …
DELLA: (*Surprised*) But that's why I'm here!
FENTON: Is she a friend of yours?
DELLA: She's my sister.
FENTON: Oh.
DELLA: You seem excited! Has something happened?
FENTON: (*Watching her*) Charles Constance is dead. He's
been murdered. He's upstairs on the floor, in
your sister's flat.
DELLA: What! I don't believe it!
FENTON: I'm telling you the truth. That's why I went down
to the phone box, to phone Scotland Yard. The
police'll be here any minute.
DELLA: Did you discover – him?

FENTON: (*Nodding*) Yes. (*Takes her by the arm*) Now look here, Miss Freeman, there's something you've got to tell me, quickly, before the police get here. What did the card mean?

DELLA: I don't know what you're talking about!

FENTON: (*With authority*) You know what I'm talking about! The card you sent to Constance, with the flowers. The Broken Horseshoe, what does it mean?

DELLA: I – I don't know.

FENTON: (*Holding her firmly by the arm*) You must know!

DELLA: I tell you, I don't. I lied to you that day at the hospital. Constance wasn't a friend of mine. I'd never even seen him …

FENTON: Then why did you send him the flowers – and that card?

DELLA: I didn't – I only delivered them.

FENTON: Who asked you to deliver them? (*A moment; her watching*) Was it your sister?

(*DELLA nods*)

FENTON: Could she have murdered Mr Constance?

DELLA: (*Tensely*) No, of course not!

FENTON: How do you know?

DELLA: Lynn couldn't do a thing like that, besides, she was very fond of Charles. (*Suddenly; suspicious*) Why did you want to see my sister?

FENTON: Constance gave me a letter and asked me to post it for him. It was addressed to a Mrs Kelsey. I wondered if, by any chance, you were Mrs Kelsey, so – I decided to deliver it and find out.

DELLA: I see.

FENTON: I wonder if you do see?

DELLA: What do you mean?

35

FENTON: I wanted to see you again. I've been wanting to see you ever since you came to the hospital that afternoon with the flowers.

(*A moment*)

DELLA: (A*voiding his eyes*) Have you still got the letter?

FENTON: Yes.

DELLA: If you give it to me, I'll see that my sister gets it.

FENTON: I'm sorry, I can't do that. I've got to hand it over to the police. In any case, it isn't exactly a letter.

(*Takes envelope and ticket from his pocket*)

FENTON: I opened it. This was inside.

(*Shows her the ticket*)

DELLA: What is it?

FENTON: It's a railway ticket.

DELLA: But why should Charles Constance want to send my sister a railway ticket?

FENTON: Supposing you tell me?

DELLA: (R*ather angry*) You think I'm mixed up in this business, don't you? You think I know why Constance was strangled and why my sister sent him that card with the Broken Horseshoe on it.

(*FENTON looks at her for a moment*)

FENTON: (N*odding*) Yes …

DELLA: Does that mean you're going to hand me over to the police?

FENTON: I'm not in a position to hand you over to anyone. It's up to you whether you go to the police or not.

DELLA: I haven't anything to go to the police about. I haven't done anything I'm ashamed of. (*Softly*) I'm just desperately worried, that's all.

FENTON: About your sister?

DELLA: Yes – partly.

FENTON: And …

DELLA: Well, stop getting yourself involved, because believe me, it's not worth it.

FENTON: In other words, you don't want me to help you.

DELLA: You can't help me, no one can help me.

FENTON: I wouldn't be too sure about that, if I were you.

(*DELLA looks at him for a moment, undecided*)

DELLA: (*About to make a suggestion*) Well ... (H*esitates*)

FENTON: Go on.

DELLA: (S*hakes her head; changing her mind*) No. It would only make things worse, much worse.

FENTON: (F*irmly*) What were you going to say?

(*DELLA hesitates again, about to speak*)

FENTON: Please ...

DELLA: I was going to say, if you'd like to meet me somewhere, later tonight, perhaps – I'll tell you about my sister and Charles Constance.

FENTON: Where would you like to meet me?

DELLA: (*A moment*) Do you know Pinelio's – in Greek Street?

FENTON: Yes, I know it. I'll see you there tonight at (*Looks at his watch*) ... ten o'clock. All right?

DELLA: (A*fter a moment*) Yes, I'll be there. (*She faces him; intently*) Then please don't tell the police anything about ... (S*he hesitates*)

FENTON: I shan't mention you to the police, if that's what you're thinking.

DELLA: No, I wasn't just thinking of myself. (*Obviously worried*) Don't tell them about the letter, about the railway ticket. Please don't.

FENTON: But I've got to tell them about the letter, otherwise they'll wonder why I came here.

DELLA: Well – please don't tell them about it until – after – tonight.

(*A long pause*)

37

FENTON: All right. I'd better get up. Now don't worry! I'll
see you at Pinelio's. Ten o'clock.
(*DELLA smiles at him*)

CUT TO: Long shot of street and Drayton Court.
*A police car brakes to a standstill. GEORGE BELLAMY and
two plain clothes men get out of the car. DELLA emerges and
gets into her car. BELLAMY looks at DELLA and realises he
has seen her before.*

CUT TO: *FENTON is standing in front of Flat 27. He looks
thoughtful. GEORGE BELLAMY and SERGEANT LEWIS
emerge from lift.*
GEORGE: Hello, Mark! This is a new experience for you,
isn't it?
FENTON: It's one I'm not very keen on.
GEORGE: Have you been up here all the time?
FENTON: Since I 'phoned you.
GEORGE: Seen anyone?
FENTON: No. The flat belongs to a Mrs Kelsey, but she's
out.
GEORGE: (*Looks at FENTON for a moment, then*) O.K. it's
take a look inside.

CUT TO: *FENTON, BELLAMY and SERGEANT LEWIS
enter the drawing room of the flat. The radio is still playing.*
GEORGE: Somebody's had a nice picnic here, by the look of
things!
(*GEORGE and the SERGEANT cross over to the body of
CHARLES CONSTANCE. GEORGE kneels down and
examines the body. FENTON stands watching them.
GEORGE rises and just catches FENTON looking at the
mirror. FENTON's expression changes*)

38

FENTON: (*Turning; casually. Nods towards CONSTANCE*) I should say he's been dead about an hour.

GEORGE: Yes. He's been strangled. Looks as if the man who did it used a scarf.

FENTON: So you already know it was a man? That's quick work!

GEORGE: Women don't usually go in for this sort of thing – Well, what's the story, Mark? How do you fit into all this?

FENTON: Well – it's really quite simple. I had a phone message from Constance this morning. He said he wasn't feeling too good and he wanted to see me. He gave me this address and I made an appointment for six o'clock. When I arrived … (*Nods towards CONSTANCE and the room generally*) … this is what I found.

GEORGE: How did you get in?

FENTON: The door was unlatched. I couldn't get a reply, but I heard the radio playing, so I just walked in.

GEORGE: (*Looking at him*) Well, that sounds simple enough. (*Casually*) How do you know the flat belongs to Mrs Kelsey?

FENTON: (*After a faint hesitation*) Constance told me.

GEORGE: Is he a friend of hers?

FENTON: I suppose he must be.

(*SERGEANT LEWIS returns from the bedroom*)

GEORGE: You've never seen her?

FENTON: No, I've told you. The flat was empty except for Constance.

GEORGE: What is it, Mark?

FENTON: Nothing.

LEWIS: You should see the bedroom, sir, it's even worse than here!

(*A pause. GEORGE lights FENTON's cigarette with lighter*)

39

GEORGE: (*Looking at the room*) Well, somebody's certainly been searching for something. (*To FENTON*) I suppose you've no idea what it was Mark?

FENTON: (*Faintly irritated*) No, of course not.

LEWIS: They've even taken the phone to pieces.

GEORGE: (*To Lewis*) Check on the rest of the flats, Lewis …

LEWIS: Yes, sir.

(*LEWIS goes towards the door*)

GEORGE: … and see if Harper's found the hall porter. If he has, bring him up here.

LEWIS: Yes, sir.

(*LEWIS goes*)

FENTON: What happens now?

GEORGE: Oh, the usual routine. We wait for the Police Surgeon and a gentleman called Foxby-Wilson. He's the finger-print expert.

FENTON: It's funny, I thought there'd be people dashing all over the place – taking photographs, checking fingerprints, asking questions.

GEORGE: That comes later. (*Smiling; facing FENTON*) Still we mustn't disappoint you. Let's start with the questions. Do you remember that girl, Mark?

FENTON: Which girl?

GEORGE: The girl who came to the hospital – the one that brought Constance the flowers.

FENTON: Yes, of course I do.

GEORGE: Have you seen her since?

FENTON: No. She telephoned on the Friday morning. I told you.

GEORGE: … What did she look like – this girl?

FENTON: You saw her.

GEORGE: Yes, but only for a moment, and I didn't take any particular notice. I thought she was a patient.

FENTON: Well, she's dark, fairly tall, good looking …

40

GEORGE: What was she wearing?

FENTON: (*Without thinking, starts to describe the outfit worn by DELLA in the previous scene*) She was wearing a grey costume and ... (*Suddenly realising his mistake*) No. She was wearing a black coat ... and a little red hat with a feather in it.

GEORGE: M'm. (*Takes a postcard size photograph out of his breast pocket*) Would you say this was the same girl?

(*FENTON takes the photograph*)

FENTON: (*Staring at the photograph*) Good Lord, no!

GEORGE: Are you sure?

FENTON: Of course I'm sure!

GEORGE: Women can disguise themselves, you know. You'd be surprised. A different hairstyle ...

FENTON: (*Handing GEORGE the photograph*) Yes, but this isn't Miss Freeman – I'm sure of it!

GEORGE: (*Accepting his word for it*) O.K. (*Takes photograph*)

(*SERGEANT LEWIS returns*)

LEWIS: The hall porter's off duty, sir. He won't be back until tomorrow. Harper and Sergeant White are checking the other flats, sir.

GEORGE: Good!

LEWIS: The doctor's arrived, sir, with Mr Foxby-Wilson. They're coming straight up.

GEORGE: Right! (*To FENTON*) There's no need for you to stay, Mark, if you don't want to. I can always get you at the hospital.

FENTON: Yes, all right.

(*He glances across at CONSTANCE and then crosses to the door*)

GEORGE: (*Following him; pleasantly*) You've told us everything, Mark – there's nothing else? Nothing you've forgotten?

FENTON: (*Avoiding GEORGE*) No, I don't think so …

GEORGE: Well, if you do remember anything, you can always give me a ring.

(*FENTON nods and goes out*)

GEORGE: Sergeant.

LEWIS: Yes, sir?

GEORGE: There's two sets of prints on this photograph – mine and Dr Fenton's. Check Fenton's with the ones you find in the flat.

LEWIS: Yes, sir. (*He looks at GEORGE; curious*) Dr Fenton's your brother-in-law, isn't he, sir?

GEORGE: Yes …

(*He looks up at the mirror, puzzled; rubs his chin*)

GEORGE: … He's my brother-in-law, Sergeant …

CUT TO: *FENTON leaving Drayton Court and walking slowly down the street. He looks worried; he hesitates for a moment, as if he is on the verge of returning to Drayton Court. He continues walking down the street.*

FENTON's VOICE: I was very worried, George. I had a shrewd suspicion that you knew I'd lied to you about Della, and I wondered if, by any chance, you'd seen her when she was leaving the flat. And there was something else that worried me. Della had referred to the fact that Constance has been strangled – but I'd never told her that, I'd only told her he'd been murdered. This meant one of two things – either someone had told her about Constance, or she'd seen the body herself.

CUT TO: FENTON's Office.

FENTON is sitting at his desk telling GEORGE the story. Same layout, clothes, etc as in the scene at the beginning of Part 1.

FENTON: When I got back to the hospital, I examined the railway ticket again – and it seemed to me just a perfectly ordinary ticket. And yet I felt sure that that's why the flat had been ransacked ...

GEORGE: (*Nodding*) Go on, Mark.

FENTON: I made up my mind not to take the ticket with me to Pinelio's.

GEORGE: Why?

FENTON: I knew that if I did, and Della asked me for it again, I might – well – I might be tempted to give it to her. I put it in an envelope and put it in this drawer.

(*He taps the drawer of his desk*)

GEORGE: Go on ...

FENTON: I left the hospital at about half past nine and picked up a taxi on the corner of Pelham Crescent. Just as I was getting into it, I had a sudden idea. I told the driver to take me to Paddington ...

CUT TO: *A taxi pulling into Paddington Railway Station. FENTON jumps out of the taxi and enters the Booking   Hall. Night.*

CUT TO: Booking Office Window, 1st Class.

FENTON stands at the window for a moment. A man moves into position at the window.

FENTON: I want a ticket to Birmingham, please – First Class, single ...

MAN: (*Taking ticket and preparing to date stamp it on machine*) Thirty-seven and ninepence …

FENTON: Thank you. Oh – er – do you think you could stamp another date on the ticket for me?

MAN: (*Hesitating*) You mean tomorrow's date?

FENTON: Er – no, not tomorrow. February 24th.

MAN: (*Surprised*) February 24th! You mean next February 24th?

FENTON: No – er – last February.

MAN: Well, I can't stamp last February 24th on it, an' even if I could it wouldn't be any good.

FENTON: Yes, I appreciate that, but –

MAN: (*Officiously*) When are you travelling?

FENTON: Well – as a matter of fact, I'm not.

MAN: You're not?

FENTON: No.

MAN: (*With sarcasm*) You want a First-Class single ticket to Birmingham, dated February 24th, but you're not going to Birmingham! Is that it?

FENTON: That's right.

MAN: Look – if you're not going to Birmingham you don't want a ticket dated February 24th or any other date. You just don't want a ticket!

FENTON: No, I don't think you see the point.

MAN: Well, once of us isn't seeing it, that's a certainty!

FENTON: Look – just give me a ticket. A single, First Class – you can put to-day's date on it if you like.

MAN: To Birmingham?

FENTON: Yes.

MAN: But you're not going to Birmingham?

FENTON: No.

MAN: (*Controlling himself; stamping the ticket*) All right! Thirty-seven and ninepence …

44

(*FENTON hands over the money. The MAN slaps down the change and the ticket. FENTON picks up his money and the ticket and leaves. The MAN is half angry, half bewildered, scratches his head, picks up a notice which says 'CLOSED' and puts it in front of the window*)

CUT TO: Interior. Pinelio's Restaurant. Night. Track in to salver in waiter's hand & track with salver to centre table on to glass of celery. PAN UP to reveal GALLEGOS.

WAITER: These are the only cigars we've got, sir. I'm sorry.

GALLEGOS: (*Looking at the box*) You've every reason to be sorry. How much are you charging for those?

WAITER: I think they're seven and six, sir.

GALLEGOS: You <u>think</u> they're seven and six?

WAITER: Yes, sir.

GALLEGOS: (*Taking a cigar from his breast pocket and handing it to the WAITER*) Well, present my compliments to the patron – and give him this. It cost me one and six – in a first-class restaurant.

WAITER: (*Surprised*) In London, sir?

GALLEGOS: Don't be naïve, my friend. I said, in a first-class restaurant.

(*FENTON enters; he is wearing his hat and coat*)

FENTON: (*To WAITER, taking off his hat and coat*) Good evening.

WAITER: Good evening, sir.

FENTON: I reserved a table for two.

WAITER: Yes, sir. (*Takes hat and coat*) Excuse me a moment, sir.

(*FENTON stands by GALLEGOS' table; takes no notice of him*)

45

GALLEGOS: (*Smiling*) Good evening, doctor.

FENTON: (*Turning*) Oh, good evening.

GALLEGOS: You don't remember me?

FENTON: No, I'm afraid I don't.

GALLEGOS: (*Rising*) Gallegos. Felix Gallegos …

FENTON: (*Politely; he doesn't remember*) Oh. Oh, yes, of course.

GALLEGOS: (*Amused*) But you still don't remember … (*Nods to the vacant chair at the table*) Will you join me for an aperitif – before your guest arrives?

FENTON: If you don't mind, I … (*Glances at his watch*) I think my friend will be here any minute, and …

GALLEGOS: (*Moving the chair round for FENTON to sit down*) You can leave me the moment she comes – I assure you. (*Turns; raising his voice*) Garçon! (*He sits down*)

(*The WAITER returns*)

WAITER: Monsieur?

GALLEGOS: An aperitif for Dr Fenton.

WAITER: Yes, sir. (*To FENTON*) What would you like, sir?

FENTON: (*Hesitating*) Well – a dry vermouth, please.

WAITER: Thank you, sir.

(*The WAITER goes. FENTON sits down facing GALLEGOS. GALLEGOS looks at FENTON, butters a biscuit, selects a piece of celery, eats. GALLEGOS doesn't speak; he smiles at FENTON. FENTON looks slightly uncomfortable. There is a pause*)

FENTON: (*Suddenly*) You know, I'm sorry, Mr Gallegos, but I still can't place you.

GALLEGOS: No?

FENTON: (*Shaking his head*) No. Were you ever a patient of mine?

46

GALLEGOS: No.

FENTON: I've seen you at the hospital, perhaps?

(*GALLEGOS shakes his head, holds up the wine glass and then drinks*)

GALLEGOS: (*Slowly, watching FENTON*) Have you been to Chipping Campden lately?

FENTON: (*Surprised*) Oh! Oh, so that's where we met! No, I'm afraid I haven't.

GALLEGOS: A delightful little place; rather commercialised, of course, especially in the summer.

FENTON: I haven't been to Chipping Campden for – oh, almost four years.

GALLEGOS: (*Nodding ... his thoughts elsewhere*) Yes ...

FENTON: Is that when we met?

(*GALLEGOS takes a cigar from his breast pocket*)

GALLEGOS: (*Preparing the cigar*) M'm?

FENTON: Is that where we met – in Chipping Campden?

GALLEGOS: (*Putting the cigar in his mouth, taking a match from the box on the table, striking the match*) No, that's not where we met, doctor.

(*The WAITER returns with the Dubonnet*)

WAITER: Your Dubonnet, sir. (*He puts the glass down in front of FENTON*)

FENTON: Thank you.

(*The WAITER goes. GALLEGOS is lighting his cigar*)

GALLEGOS: (*Nodding towards the Dubonnet*) I'm glad to see you don't pollute it with gin. Whenever I think of England, I always think of gin and Worcester sauce. (*Amused*) Not together, of course.

(*GALLEGOS looks at his cigar, examines it*)

FENTON: (*After a pause, watching GALLEGOS*) We've never met before, have we?

GALLEGOS: (*Looking up from his cigar, smiling*) No.

47

FENTON: Did Miss Freeman send you?

GALLEGOS: (*Ignoring the question, watching FENTON*)
            Cherry Hill Cottage, Stratford Road, Chipping
            Campden. Am I correct?

FENTON: That's where I was born – yes.

GALLEGOS: On September 4th, 1913? Correct?

FENTON: Yes.

GALLEGOS: You know, you don't look your age, doctor. I
            should have said thirty-two – thirty-three
            perhaps – no more …

FENTON: Look here, who the devil are you – and what's
            this all about?

GALLEGOS: Your father was a metallurgical chemist, he
            worked for a Coventry firm called Smedley and
            Bristow. His name was Browning. Fenton was
            your Mother's maiden name. You changed
            your name by deed poll in October, 1934.
            Correct?

FENTON: (*After a moment*) You still haven't answered
            my question, Mr Gallegos.

GALLEGOS: About Miss Freeman?

FENTON: Yes.

(*The WAITER appears*)

GALLEGOS: Della – that's Miss Freeman – asked me to tell
            you that unfortunately, owing to a previous
            engagement, she …

WAITER: Excuse me m'sieur.

GALLEGOS: Yes? What is it?

WAITER: (*To FENTON*) Mr Fenton of St Mathew's
            Hospital?

FENTON: Yes?

WAITER: You're wanted on the telephone, sir.

FENTON: Who wants me?

WAITER: The gentleman did not say, sir.

FENTON: (*Staring at GALLEGOS, rising*) All right. Where's the phone?

WAITER: (*Nodding*) In the alcove, sir.

(*FENTON stands; looks down at GALLEGOS for a moment*)

FENTON: Don't go away, Mr Gallegos.

GALLEGOS: I shall be here, doctor. You can depend on it.

(*FENTON crosses to the curtained alcove on the right of the table. There is a wall telephone with a coin-box in the alcove. Current theatre list is pinned to the wall near the telephone*)

FENTON: (*Lifting receiver*) Hello?

CRAIG's VOICE: (*On phone*) Is that you, Fenton? This is Craig. ...

FENTON: Oh, hello, Craig?

CRAIG's VOICE: Sorry to ring you but Robertson has just phoned to say he has flu and there's no one on call for emergency.

FENTON: (*Curtly*) Well, get hold of Turner!

CRAIG's VOICE: Turner's dining out somewhere and the idiot didn't leave a phone number.

FENTON: You bet he didn't! I'm the idiot, not Turner! All right, Craig, I'll be here at this number for the next half hour then I'll come to the hospital.

(*GALLEGOS is leaning forward slightly, across the table, touching the glass of Dubonnet. He leans back in his chair and sits smoking his cigar. FENTON returns to the table. He looks annoyed*)

GALLEGOS: You see, I'm still here.

FENTON: (*Curtly*) Now supposing you get to the point, Mr Gallesco.

GALLEGOS: (*Correcting him*) Gallegos.

FENTON: All right, Gallegos, or whatever your name is!

GALLEGOS: (*Smiling, indicating the chair*) Which particular point would you like me to get to?

49

FENTON: (*Sitting down*) You can start with Miss Freeman. Why didn't she come here tonight? She gave me her word she would.

GALLEGOS: She – changed her mind. It's a female prerogative. I tried to persuade her to come, but – it was quite impossible.

FENTON: How well do you know Miss Freeman?

GALLEGOS: She's a protégé of mine.

FENTON: What do you mean – protégé?

GALLEGOS: It's a simple word. It only has one meaning. (*Smiling*) But don't let's talk about Miss Freeman; let's talk about you … Or, if you prefer it, about your father.

FENTON: (*A moment*) What about my father?

GALLEGOS: He served a term of imprisonment – six years in fact – for embezzlement. (*He looks at his cigar*) That's probably why you changed your name.

FENTON: There's no probability about it – that's why I did change my name.

GALLEGOS: (*Looking up*) Do they know about your father at the hospital?

FENTON: I imagine so. The whole world knows about him. I have a press cutting book if you'd care to borrow it any time.

(*FENTON is quite calm but a shade embarrassed. He picks up the glass and drinks. GALLEGOS looks at FENTON for a moment and then suddenly starts to laugh*)

GALLEGOS: You're bluffing, Mr Fenton. They don't know about your father at the hospital. Very few people know.

(*FENTON drinks the rest of the Dubonnet and puts the glass down. He looks at GALLEGOS with obvious contempt*)

50

FENTON: Forgive me if I stare. It's the first time I've ever met a blackmailer.

GALLEGOS: Don't be too impressed. I'm an amateur. Blackmail, so far as I'm concerned, is merely a means to an end.

(*FENTON takes out his wallet and extracts a railway ticket. He shows it to GALLEGOS*)

FENTON: Is this what you want?

GALLEGOS: Yes.

FENTON: What's your price?

GALLEGOS: (*Slowly*) Am I to understand that you are prepared to sell that ticket?

FENTON: Why not?

GALLEGOS: This is something I didn't bargain for! (*Confidentially*) Do we, by any chance, talk the same language?

FENTON: What language do you talk?

GALLEGOS: I'll give you a hundred pounds for it.

FENTON: (*Holding up the ticket*) For this?

GALLEGOS: Yes.

FENTON: I warn you, it's just an ordinary railway ticket, from London to Birmingham.

GALLEGOS: (*Smiling*) I know that, but I'll give you one hundred pounds for it – cash. What do you say?

FENTON: (*Holding the bridge of his nose; he is feeling slightly dizzy*) The ticket's yours, Mr Gallegos – but not for a hundred pounds.

GALLEGOS: What do you mean?

FENTON: (*Rubbing his hand across his eyes*) Why didn't Miss Freeman keep her appointment? Who murdered Charles Constance? And what's … the … significance … of … the … Broken Horseshoe.

GALLEGOS: (*Watching FENTON*) If I answer those questions, will you give me the ticket?

FENTON: (*Obviously feeling ill*) Yes …

GALLEGOS: (*Slowly; watching FENTON*) I told you why Della didn't keep the appointment. She – had – a – previous engagement. Are you feeling all right?

FENTON: (*His hand over his eyes*) No, I'm not. (*He tries to rise from the table*)

GALLEGOS: I shouldn't get up.

FENTON: (*Holding the table*) What is it? I feel as if the room's going round … (*He steadies himself against the table*)

(*The WAITER arrives*)

WAITER: Is anything the matter, sir?

GALLEGOS: Fetch some water – iced water.

WAITER: Yes, sir.

(*The WAITER goes*)

FENTON: (*Still holding the table, looking down at GALLEGOS*) You put something in my drink, didn't you?

GALLEGOS: (*Nodding; quite calm*) Sit down. There's nothing to worry about. You'll be all right in half an hour.

(*FENTON sits down again. He holds his head in his hands. GALLEGOS leans forward and picks up the railway ticket*)

GALLEGOS: I'll take care of this. (*He puts the ticket in his pocket and then picks up FENTON's wallet*) You'd better put this in your pocket.

(*FENTON covers his eyes with his hands, and leans forward, resting on the table. The WAITER returns carrying a glass of iced water and a wine glass*)

GALLEGOS: (*Rising; handing the WAITER a five-pound note*) Keep the change, my friend.

52

WAITER: (*Surprised*) Thank you, sir.

GALLEGOS: (*Moving towards the door; nods towards the table*) There's nothing to worry about. He gets these dizzy spells. He'll be all right in half an hour. See he drinks plenty of iced water.

WAITER: (*Puzzled, surprised that GALLEGOS is leaving*) Yes, sir. Au revoir m'sieur.

(*The WAITER stares at GALLEGOS as he leaves, then moves across to the table. He pours out a glass of water. After an unsuccessful attempt, FENTON just manages to lift the glass and drink. He puts down the glass*)

FENTON's VOICE: (*Over action*) Gallegos was right about the iced water, it certainly made me feel better. But it took almost an hour for the effect of the chloral to wear off ...

(*The WAITER pours another glass of water*)

FENTON's VOICE: When I felt well enough to stand, I asked the waiter to get me a taxi. I remembered what Craig had said – about Robertson being ill – and I wanted to get back to the hospital.

(*FENTON drinks another glass of water*)

CUT TO: A ward of St Matthew's Hospital. There are nurses, patients, etc.

FENTON's VOICE: It was half past eleven when I arrived at St Matthew's.

CUT TO: A small changing room in the hospital. There are lockers, wash-hand basins, roller towels, shelf with face towels, hairbrushes, comb, eau-de-cologne etc.

53

DR CRAIG has just finished washing, and he is drying his face on a towel. FENTON enters. He is wearing his outdoor clothes. During the following scene he changes into his surgeon's coat and places his coat and hat in his locker.

CRAIG: Hello, Fenton!

FENTON: Sorry I'm late. How's Robertson?

CRAIG: He's off tonight. Turner's doing a spot of duty for a change.

FENTON: I thought you couldn't get hold of him.

CRAIG: Who?

FENTON: Turner.

CRAIG: (*Combing his hair*) What d'ye, mean? I never said we couldn't get hold of him.

FENTON: But you did. You said he was dining out and you hadn't got his phone number.

CRAIG: (*Staring at FENTON*) I did?

FENTON: Yes.

CRAIG: When?

FENTON: (*A shade irritated*) When you spoke to me on the phone. Damn it man, that's why I'm here, because you couldn't reach Turner!

CRAIG: (*Facing him; amazed*) I spoke to you on the telephone?

FENTON: Yes.

CRAIG: Tonight?

FENTON: Yes.

CRAIG: (*Taking his arm*) Fenton, are you feeling all right?

FENTON: No, I'm not feeling all right! I'm feeling damn bad, but what's that got to do with it?

CRAIG: It seems to me it's got a great deal to do with it! (*Shaking his head*) I didn't phone you tonight. I haven't been near a phone. If you must know, I've been having a good old heart to heart with

54

Armitage. He now thinks we don't know anything.

FENTON: Craig, are you serious? Didn't you phone me?

CRAIG: (*Amused*) Of course I didn't!

FENTON: (*Thoughtfully*) Well, that's extraordinary! It was your voice. I'd swear it was your voice!

CRAIG: Well, if you don't believe me, go and have a word with Turner.

FENTON: (*After a moment, hesitatingly*) This isn't a leg pull, is it?

CRAIG: Of course it isn't a leg pull! I may have a queer sense of humour, but I don't ring people up when they're off duty. In any case, we're full strength tonight. I'm here, Turner's here, Gillespie's here, there's only you and Robertson off duty.

FENTON: (*Thoughtfully*) Yes … yes, of course. (*Looks up*) Sorry, Craig. (*Smiles*) Sorry I was rude just now.

CRAIG: That's all right, old boy. I should take it easy for a day or two. Don't overdo things …

(*He looks at FENTON. He is puzzled, he walks towards the camera using it as a mirror and brushes his hair*)

CUT TO: FENTON's office.

FENTON is sitting at the desk. Telling GEORGE the story. Same lay-out, clothes etc as before. GEORGE looks serious.

FENTON: That's the whole story, George. Up to date …

GEORGE: Not quite the whole story. (*He looks at FENTON; quietly*) Tell me more about this man Gallegos. What did he look like?

FENTON: He was dark, stout, spoke with an accent. It's difficult to say how old he was. Fifty, perhaps.

GEORGE: Would you recognise him again?

FENTON: Yes, of course.

GEORGE: Mark, why didn't you tell me about the mirror and the broken horseshoe?

FENTON: I've told you why, I – promised Della I wouldn't say anything until I'd seen her at Pinelio's.

GEORGE: It's surprising what a pretty face can do, isn't it?

FENTON: What do you mean?

GEORGE: She made a fool out of you.

FENTON: (*Angry*) All right, she made a fool out of me!

GEORGE: (*After a moment*) Have you got the railway ticket?

(*FENTON opens the drawer in the desk and takes out an envelope. He passes it to GEORGE*)

GEORGE: (*Opening it and looking at the ticket*) Is this the one that Constance gave you?

FENTON: Yes.

(*GEORGE studies the ticket*)

FENTON: (*After a pause*) George – don't you believe what I've told you this afternoon?

GEORGE: I believed you yesterday, when you said it was Constance who asked you to go to the flat.

FENTON: Yes, but don't you see, I couldn't tell you about the ticket, not until …

GEORGE: (*Interrupting; sceptical*) Not until you'd seen Miss Freeman. I get your point.

FENTON: (*Tensely*) You don't believe me, do you?

(*GEORGE looks at FENTON for a moment and then looks down at the ticket he is holding*)

GEORGE: (*After a moment, not looking at FENTON*) I think you said that, when you went to the flat you were wearing gloves. Is that right?

FENTON: Yes.

GEORGE: Did you take them off?

FENTON: Only in the phone box.

GEORGE: (*Looking up, at FENTON*) You were wearing gloves all the time you were in the flat alone?

(*FENTON nods*)

GEORGE: You're sure about that?

FENTON: Quite sure.

(*GEORGE looks down again at the ticket; he is examining it*)

FENTON: You still haven't answered my question. Do you believe my story?

(*GEORGE looks up. After a pause, he shakes his head. He looks very worried*)

GEORGE: No.

FENTON: (*Tensely*) Why not?

GEORGE: Because after you left the flat, we found fingerprints near the dead man. (*He looks straight at FENTON*) They were yours, Mark …

END OF PART TWO

Part Three:

MISS JACKIE LEROY

OPEN TO: Main entrance of St Matthew's Hospital. A busy scene of nurses, doctors, medical students, patients etc passing to and fro.

CUT TO: FENTON's Office.

GEORGE is looking down at the   railway ticket which is in his hand.

GEORGE: (*After a moment, not looking at FENTON*) I think you said that, when you went to the flat you were wearing gloves. Is that right?

FENTON: Yes.

GEORGE: Did you take them off?

FENTON: Only in the phone box.

GEORGE: (*Looking up, at FENTON*) You were wearing gloves   all the time you were in the flat alone?

(*FENTON nods*)

GEORGE: You're sure about that?

FENTON: Quite sure.

(*GEORGE looks down again at the ticket; he is examining it*)

FENTON: You still haven't answered my question. Do you believe my story?

(*GEORGE looks up. After a pause, he shakes his head. He looks very worried*)

GEORGE: No.

FENTON: (*Tensely*) Why not?

GEORGE: Because after you left the flat, we found fingerprints near the dead man. (*He looks straight at FENTON*) They were yours, Mark …

FENTON: Mine?

GEORGE: They were yours.

FENTON: But that's impossible!

GEORGE: We compared them with the ones on the photograph. They were identical.

61

FENTON: I don't care what you compared them with! I tell you I didn't touch anything in the flat, and anyhow, I was wearing gloves!

(*GEORGE moves behind FENTON and stands with his back to him*)

GEORGE: (*Turning to FENTON*) Mark, it's no use! We found Constance's watch, wallet and cigarette lighter. His initials and fingerprints were on all three and your prints were on the lighter.

FENTON: I didn't even see his cigarette lighter!

GEORGE: Did you see the watch or wallet?

FENTON: I saw the wallet, yes, it was by the side of the body – but I didn't touch it. (*Irritatedly, swinging round in his chair*) You don't believe me.

GEORGE: It isn't a question of what I believe.

FENTON: Well, if I can't convince you, I'm not likely to convince the rest of Scotland Yard, am I?

GEORGE: (*Turning towards the door*) Give me your statement and I'll give it to the Superintendent. We'll see what he makes of it.

FENTON: (*Rises*) George, just a minute! You can't go like this. Why should I lie to you?

GEORGE: You lied to me yesterday, Mark! You said that Constance had phoned you and asked you to see him at Drayton Court.

FENTON: But I've explained why I did that. I promised Della Freeman that I wouldn't say anything until …

GEORGE: (*Interrupting; angry*) How do I know that you're still not covering up for Della Freeman? (*With a contemptuous gesture*) How do I know that this story of yours isn't a pack of lies from start to finish?

FENTON: You don't know! You've got to accept my word for it.

GEORGE: (*Facing FENTON*) Well, frankly, I'm not pepared to.

FENTON: Then there's nothing more to be said.

(*FENTON goes to the door and unlocks it. He returns to his desk and sits. He clicks up the switch on the house phone*)

GEORGE: Look, you know I want to give you every chance. Supposing we go over this story of yours? (*He sits*) A complete stranger to you called Charles Constance is knocked down by a car. He's brought to the hospital, you operate, and he gets better. Della Freeman comes to the hospital with some flowers for Constance and she leaves a card with a picture of a broken horseshoe on it. But Constance says that he's never heard of Della and he's apparently puzzled by the horseshoe. When he leaves the hospital, he gives you a letter, or rather an envelope containing a railway ticket addressed to a Mrs Kelsey (*With a shrug*) Why he should do that I can't imagine.

FENTON: Anyway, I take the envelope to Mrs Kelsey's flat, and find the body of Charles Constance.

GEORGE: Yes, that's just the beginning, Mark! Even without the sign on the mirror, and your fingerprints on the lighter – it's quite a story! Frankly, do you think it's convincing?

FENTON: I don't care whether it's convincing or not. It's the truth!

GEORGE: Why did Constance give you the letter – why didn't he post it?

FENTON: I don't know why!

GEORGE: (*A shrug*) All right, but why didn't you post it – instead of taking it to the flat?

63

FENTON: I was hoping to see Miss Freeman!

GEORGE: Well, you saw her! Did she explain about the flowers, or the railway ticket, or the broken horseshoe?

FENTON: (*Exasperated*) I've told you what happened! She asked me to meet her at Pinelio's, but when I got there Gallegos was waiting for me. He tried to get the railway ticket. (*Suddenly*) Look, George – I'm a doctor, not a detective. I don't know why Constance was murdered and I don't know who murdered him. You'd better give my statement to the Superintendent – perhaps he's got more imagination.

(*Sound on house phone. GEORGE rises*)

GEORGE: He'll certainly need it! I'll give you a ring some time tonight. We shall probably want you to come down to the Yard.

FENTON: (*Weary*) Yes, all right.

(*GEORGE goes out. FENTON turns towards the house phone, touches key*)

FENTON: (*On house phone*) Yes, all right. Send her along.

(*FENTON goes to filing cabinet*)

CUT TO: *GEORGE walks slowly down the corridor, away from FENTON's office, towards the main hall of the hospital. Nurses, medical students etc are looking at a notice board. GEORGE looks worried; there is an unlit pipe in his mouth. He stops and takes a box of matches out of his pocket. Immediately behind where he is standing there is a large notice board which carries the usual advertisements: "Lost" and "Found" articles; news of various hospital functions etc. As he lights his pipe, GEORGE glances casually across at the notice board; hesitates; takes the pipe*

from his mouth; moves closer to the board. He reads a typed
postcard   which is pinned to the board. The card reads:
'LOST'
"Silver cigarette lighter. The maker's name
Dauphin et Cie – is stamped on the base.
If you have any information concerning this
please communicate
with the Secretary or with Mark Fenton"

GEORGE turns, looks back down the corridor towards the
door of FENTON's office. He puts the pipe back in his mouth;
looks very thoughtful.

CUT TO: FENTON's Office.
FENTON is standing by the filing cabinet. There is a knock
and he turns towards the door. The door opens and JACKIE
LEROY pops her head into the room.
JACKIE: Hello.
FENTON: Do come in, Miss Leroy! I'm sorry to have kept
you waiting.
(*JACKIE enters. She is an expensively over-dressed,*
glamorous barmaid: wears a black dress, a great deal   of
jewellery, and a fox stole. She has been forty for six years)
JACKIE: That's all right, doctor! My, you look under the
weather! What have you been doing, burning the
candle at three ends? (*Laughing*) I'll bet you
haven't! You work too hard. You want to relax a
bit. Enjoy yourself more. Look at me …
FENTON: You're looking very much better … but you might
have put on a little weight.
(*JACKIE sits in the armchair and reveals her nylons*)
JACKIE: (*Taking off her stole*) Don't rub it in for Pete's
sake!
FENTON: (*Facing her*) Well, how have you been feeling?

JACKIE: Much better! I have really, I've felt ever so much better this past week.

FENTON: Any of those dizzy spells?

JACKIE: No, not one. Oh, except on Tuesday night when my gentleman friend – yes, well I don't suppose that counts.

FENTON: What about the tablets? Have you taken them?

JACKIE: Yes.

FENTON: Regularly?

JACKIE: Yes. They're much nicer than the first lot you gave me.

FENTON: Good. We'll let's have a look at you.

JACKIE: Do you want me to undress?

FENTON: No, there's no need for that.

JACKIE: You didn't come to my party last Tuesday, doctor. I sent you an invitation.

FENTON: Yes, I know you did. It was very kind of you. I'm afraid parties aren't much in my line.

JACKIE: Oh.

(*A pause; FENTON arranges his apparatus*)

JACKIE: Are you a bachelor?

FENTON: Yes.

JACKIE: Well, why don't you like parties?

FENTON: Why didn't you like the first lot of tablets I gave you?

JACKIE: I told you. They made my mouth dry.

FENTON: Exactly. Now sit back in the chair. Just relax.

(*JACKIE relaxes. FENTON squeezes the bulb; watches apparatus. A pause*)

JACKIE: Have you got a girl friend?

FENTON: (*Pleased*) Ah! (*Looks up at JACKIE*) I'm sorry, you asked me a question just now?

JACKIE: I asked you if you'd got a girl friend?

66

FENTON: No, I haven't. And I'm delighted to say you are doing splendidly on these new pills. Continue taking them but we can reduce the dose and I shan't need to see you for about three months. You must report regularly to the laboratory for your blood count – they'll let you know if it's abnormal.

(*As he talks FENTON moves his fingers over her thyroid and examines her hands*)

JACKIE: (*Fastening her sleeve*) Well, hadn't I better pop in one day, you know – just for a check-up?

FENTON: I don't think so. If you get those dizzy spells again, or start losing weight, give me a ring.

JACKIE: Give you a ring! I'll be on the doorsteps!

(*FENTON laughs*)

FENTON: How many tablets have you got left?

JACKIE: I think there's two.

FENTON: I'd better give you another prescription. (*He starts to write prescription on pad*)

JACKIE: You've made a big difference to me – you have really. I'm ever so grateful.

(*She takes out her powder compact: does her face*)

JACKIE: That other quack I went to! I told you about him, didn't I?

FENTON: (*Nodding his head*) Yes, you did.

JACKIE: He stuck so many needles in me! All over the place! I was like a pin-cushion. I said to him one day, what is this – a game of darts?

(*FENTON hands her the prescription; she rises and crosses to the desk*)

FENTON: I've given you a prescription for some more thiouracil tablets: take one at night, every other day.

JACKIE: Okedoke!

FENTON: And don't drink too much. (*Smiling*) In any case, it's bad for the figure.

JACKIE: Oh, so you have noticed my figure?

FENTON: Yes. How much do you weigh?

JACKIE: About nine stone.

FENTON: You don't look like nine stone to me.

JACKIE: Yes, I know. I've always carried my weight very well. My gentleman friend says … Here, what do you mean, I don't look nine stone?

FENTON: (*Looking at her closely*) I should have said ten: ten and a half perhaps.

JACKIE: Oh, you would, would you? Ten and a half! (*Pulls her dress tighter*) I must look like the side of a house!

(*FENTON rises and crosses in front of the desk*)

FENTON: Well, before you leave ask sister to weigh you. If you continue gaining at this rate we'll have to put you on a diet.

JACKIE: You can put me on it, duckie – but you can't keep me on it. Do you know what trouble is? Chocs! It's terrible. I never stop … Honest, I never stop eating them.

FENTON: Can you get them all right?

JACKIE: (*Amused*) Get them? Chocolates? Don't be silly, of course I can get them!

FENTON: Well, you are very lucky.

JACKIE: Look, if you ever want anything in that line – chocolates, whisky …

FENTON: (*Laughing at her*) I'll get in touch.

JACKIE: No, I'm serious. Honestly. You've been a very good friend to me. I can get you anything you want. Chocolates, whisky, nylons for the girl friend – Oh, you haven't got a girlfriend, have

68

you? Well, I'll even get you a girlfriend if you feel like it!

(*FENTON takes Jackie by the arm and leads her towards the door*)

FENTON: (*Amused*) Miss Leroy, I don't believe a word you say! I'll bet you're the most respectable woman in London.

JACKIE: (*Shocked*) Well! That's a nice thing to say to anybody, I must say!

(*CRAIG enters*)

CRAIG: Fenton, I'd be awfully grateful if you'd have a word with Armitage. (*Stops; stares at JACKIE*) Why, hello, Jackie!

JACKIE: (*Also surprised*) Hello, Scottie!

(*CRAIG is obviously embarrassed by the presence of JACKIE in FENTON's office*)

FENTON: (*Amused*) Do you two know each other?

JACKIE: We met at a party about a week ago. (*Smiles at CRAIG*) Didn't we, Scottie?

CRAIG: Er – yes.

JACKIE: Do you work here? (*He gives an embarrassed nod. JACKIE is surprised at the idea*) Are you a doctor?

CRAIG: I'm afraid so.

JACKIE: Well, I never. Would you believe it? I never dreamt you were a doctor. That was quite a jolly little party, wasn't it?

CRAIG: Er – yes, I suppose it was.

JACKIE: How long have you known Bubbles?

CRAIG: Oh, er – about six or seven weeks, I suppose. (*To FENTON*) You see, Fenton, it's a friend of my sister's; she had a little birthday party. Just one of those quiet, friendly sort of – you know.

FENTON: (*Nods*) Yes, I know.

JACKIE: So that's your idea of a quiet friendly little party!

CRAIG: Er – yes.

JACKIE: Well! …

CRAIG: I suppose it did get a wee bit rowdy, towards the end.

JACKIE: (*Significantly*) Just a wee bit!

(*CRAIG looks at FENTON. He is painfully embarrased*)

JACKIE: (*To FENTON*) I'd better be going or you'll be treating <u>him</u> for shock.

FENTON: (*Opening the door for her*) Good-bye, Miss Leroy. Don't forget what I told you.

JACKIE: Don't forget what I told you! Bye, bye, Scottie!

CRAIG: Good-bye.

(*JACKIE goes*)

CRAIG: (*Quickly, before FENTON speaks*) Look, Fenton. I don't want you to get the wrong impression about that party. So far as I was concerned -

FENTON: (*Interrupting*) My dear fellow – it's nothing to do with me.

CRAIG: Yes, I know. But, damn it all, the way she was talking you'd imagine it was some kind of orgy!

FENTON: Forget it, Craig!

(*CRAIG sits on the arm of the armchair*)

CRAIG: (*Laughing*) How long have you known her?

FENTON: She came to me about a month ago; she's moderately hyperthyroid.

CRAIG: That doesn't completely surprise me. My word, she's a character! She's not a fool though, don't run away with that idea.

FENTON: I never thought she was. Tell me; is she as black as she makes herself out to be?

CRAIG: Well, it all depends what you mean. She knows plenty of shady customers, there's no doubt about that. (*Rises and crosses to FENTON*) But

I'll tell you one thing. If I was in trouble, I mean real, serious trouble – with the police for instance - I'd go straight to Jackie.

FENTON: Why?

CRAIG: Because she knows exactly what's going on in this town, and what she doesn't know she very soon finds out.

FENTON: Well, she certainly seems to have impressed you, Craig!

CRAIG: Aye. Of course I may be prejudiced. (*Smiles at FENTON*) She sent me four bottles of Scotch.

FENTON: (*laughs*) Come along, let's have a look at Armitage.

(*CRAIG stands on one side for FENTON to pass him*)

FENTON: After you – Scottie.

(*CRAIG gives him a dirty look*)

CUT TO: Interior Hospital. Nurses, hospital personnel passing to and fro.

SISTER ROGERS appears and walks down the corridor: she is carrying a sheaf of papers, a small bottle, and a large X-ray envelope. FENTON comes out of his office. He is wearing his overcoat and carrying his hat and gloves. He closes the door behind him and smiles at the Sister. She stops.

SISTER: Are you just off, Mr Fenton?

FENTON: Yes. (*Nods at envelope*) Is that the Dixon X-ray?

(*SISTER nods*)

FENTON: Has Dr Gillespie seen it?

SISTER: Yes, he's just seen it.

FENTON: Well?

SISTER: He thinks there has been some collapse in that right lower lobe, but he isn't certain and was suggesting having some laterals done.

FENTON: I'd like Sir Gilbert to have a look at that woman. I'm not too happy about her, Sister.

SISTER: No. Her little boy came to see her yesterday. He's a nice child: might almost be her double.

(*FENTON looks thoughtful; nods*)

FENTON: I'm off duty tomorrow, Matron. I'll see you on Wednesday morning.

SISTER: Good night, Mr Fenton.

FENTON: Good night.

CUT TO: *FENTON leaving the main entrance of the hospital. He walks down the steps, hesitates, stands for a moment looking up at the sky. There is a MAN standing on the kerb, reading a   newspaper. He gives FENTON a casual glance and   then goes on reading his paper. FENTON suddenly makes up his mind to walk; puts on his gloves; crosses the road. The MAN lowers his newspaper; follows FENTON across the road.*

CUT TO: Exterior, front window of a small tobacconist's shop.

The MAN is looking in the shop window. He is smoking a cigarette; carries his newspaper under his arm. FENTON comes out of the shop with a packet of cigarettes in his hand. He doesn't notice the MAN. FENTON strolls down the road; the MAN remains behind, still looking in the shop window. After a moment he turns and follows FENTON.

CUT TO: The sitting room of FENTON's flat.

It is a large well-furnished room with full length curtains draped over the window. The curtains are drawn and the lights on. A drinks table, easy chairs, bookshelves, writing desk, telephone, etc. There are three doors. One to the bathroom, one to the main bedroom and one through an alcove to the hall.

DELLA FREEMAN enters from the bedroom; she looks tense and alert and is conducting an unsuccessful search for the railway ticket. She stares at the desk, at the table, then suddenly crosses to the bookshelf and takes down the first volume of a collection. She quickly searches the book, flicking the pages. She replaces the book and takes down the next volume. She is searching the third volume when she suddenly stops and turns towards the alcove. She has obviously heard something; she hurriedly replaces the book. DELLA looks about her; frightened; uncertain what to do or where to go. She switches off the lights.

FENTON enters the flat, closes the front door behind him, placing the keys in his pocket. He switches on the light. There is no sign of DELLA. He takes off his overcoat and crosses into the bedroom.

Slowly, cautiously, DELLA appears from behind the curtain. She suddenly senses that FENTON is returning and she moves behind the curtain again.

FENTON returns from the bedroom. He has discarded his overcoat and the jacket and his suit. He goes into the bathroom and turns on the light. Through the half open door, we see a silhouette of FENTON preparing his bath. There is the sound of running water.

FENTON returns, unfastening his collar, taking off his tie. He looks round the room. Notices that the curtains are drawn. He crosses and is about to pull the curtain cord when the telephone bell starts ringing. FENTON hesitates; withdraws his hand. Turns, crosses and lifts the receiver.

73

FENTON: (*On phone*) Hello? Oh, hello George. Do you want me to come down to the Yard? I'm not doing anything. I'm just going to have a bath. (*Pause*) Yes, all right, I'll see you here in twenty minutes.

FENTON replaces the receiver and stands for a moment looking down at the telephone. He turns, hesitates, then suddenly decides to go into the bathroom. Through the half-open door of the bathroom we see the silhouette of FENTON feeling the water and turning the hot water tap.

DELLA emerges from behind the curtain and, with her eyes on the bathroom door, passes swiftly over to the alcove and goes out.

We see the silhouette of FENTON taking off his shirt and preparing for his bath.

CUT TO: The same. Interior of FENTON's flat. Later.
The doorbell rings and FENTON answers it. GEORGE is standing outside.
GEORGE: (*Smiling*) Sorry if I've got you out of the bath.
FENTON: That's all right. Come in.
(*They enter*)
FENTON: What did you want to see me about?
GEORGE: I'm sorry about this afternoon. I'm afraid I lost my temper.
(*FENTON crosses to the drinks table*)
FENTON: Well, if it comes to that, we both did. Would you like a drink?
(*GEORGE puts his hat down and unfastens his coat*)
GEORGE: Yes, as a matter of fact, I would.
(*FENTON pours whisky into glass*)
FENTON: Soda?

74

GEORGE: Thank you.

(*FENTON adds soda and hands GEORGE his drink*)

GEORGE: Aren't you having one?

FENTON: Not just at the moment …

GEORGE: (*Raising his glass*) Well – cheers.

(*GEORGE drinks. A pause*)

FENTON: Well, what happened? Did the Superintendent convince you that my story wasn't exactly a pack of lies?

GEORGE: (*Shaking his head*) No. (*Looks straight at FENTON; amused*) You are a prize chump!

FENTON: What do you mean?

GEORGE: Why didn't you tell me that you'd lost your cigarette lighter?

FENTON: (*Puzzled*) My cigarette lighter?

GEORGE: Yes.

FENTON: Look, I had a pretty hard morning at the hospital and a distinctly unpleasant afternoon. I'm not in the mood for riddles.

GEORGE: (*Ignoring his remark*) When did you lose your lighter?

FENTON: (*Impatiently*) Oh, about a fortnight ago, I suppose.

GEORGE: Here, or at the hospital?

FENTON: I don't know where I lost it. It might have been here; it might have been at the hospital. It'll turn up.

(*GEORGE takes a cigarette lighter out of his pocket and holds it out towards FENTON on the palm of his hand*)

GEORGE: It has.

FENTON: Well, I'm blowed. Where on earth did you find it?

(*GEORGE suddenly tosses the lighter over on the palm of his hand; the other side has the initials "CC" embossed on it*)

GEORGE: We found it by the body of Charles Constance. This is the lighter I told you about; the one with your fingerprints on it.

FENTON: (*Taking the lighter from GEORGE*) But it's exactly like mine! If it wasn't for the initials …

GEORGE: It is yours. (*He points to the lighter*) The monogram's new; there's a doubt whether it's been on the lighter more than forty-eight hours.

FENTON: (*Puzzled*) But I don't understand.

GEORGE: It's quite simple. Somebody took your lighter, had the initials inscribed on it, then planted it by the side of the body. When we found it, naturally we assumed it belonged to Constance!

(*FENTON crosses to the table and takes a cigarette from the box*)

FENTON: I see. (*Turning*) George, you think it was Della Freeman that made it look as if I'd murdered Constance?

GEORGE: I think it might have been her – yes. When did you last see her?

FENTON: I told you. Yesterday evening, at the flat. I had an appointment with her at Pinelio's but she didn't keep it.

GEORGE: You haven't seen her since?

FENTON: (*Lighting cigarette*) No.

GEORGE: Has she phoned you?

FENTON: No.

(*A pause*)

GEORGE: Are you in love with her, Mark?

FENTON: (*Faintly irritated by the question*) Dammit, I've only seen her twice.

GEORGE: Well, if you're not, you're certainly infatuated.

FENTON: All right. I'm infatuated.

GEORGE: (*Holding out his hand*) I shall have to keep the lighter – for the time being at any rate.

FENTON: Yes, of course. (*Hands the lighter to GEORGE*)

GEORGE: When I realised what has happened – (*Holding lighter*) about this, I mean, I went over your statement again.

FENTON: Well?

GEORGE: Somehow, it didn't seem quite so far-fetched.

FENTON: Careful, George, or before you know where you are you'll find yourself believing in it!

GEORGE: Mark, supposing you had to choose between us and Della Freeman.

FENTON: Don't be ridiculous. If she's murdered Charles Constance then so far as I'm concerned, she's got to face the music. (*Shaking his head*) From now on, I'm not covering up for anybody. I've learnt my lesson.

GEORGE: (*Smiling*) Good.

FENTON: (*Facing GEORGE*) Now, supposing you tell me what this business is all about?

GEORGE: What makes you think we know what it's all about?

FENTON: Don't you?

GEORGE: Well, up to a point. But we haven't got all the pieces together, not yet, not by a long chalk. There's Mrs Kelsey for instance. We don't seem to be able to get a line on her.

FENTON: Hasn't she showed up?

GEORGE: No.

FENTON: What about the flat?

GEORGE: It's a furnished flat – on a three months' lease. The extraordinary thing is most of the tenants don't seem to have set eyes on Mrs Kelsey.

FENTON: That doesn't sound exactly hopeful.

77

GEORGE: No. I'm very interested in that railway ticket …

(*The telephone starts to ring*)

FENTON: Excuse me.

(*FENTON crosses to the desk and picks up the receiver*)

FENTON: (*On phone*) Hello? … Yes? Speaking … Yes, Inspector Bellamy is here. Do you want to have a word with him? …Hold on. (*To GEORGE*) It's for you.

(*GEORGE crosses and takes the phone from FENTON*)

GEORGE: It'll be the Yard. I left word I'd be here if they wanted me.

(*FENTON unties his dressing-gown and goes into the bedroom to change*)

GEORGE: (*On phone*) Hello?

CUT TO: Inside a telephone box.

SERGEANT WALL is making a call.

WALL: (*On phone*) Is you that, Inspector? … This is Sergeant Wall, sir … I trailed Dr Fenton from the hospital, sir. The girl was in the flat waiting for him …That girl, sir – the one you described, name of Freeman … He must have had an appointment with her, sir. She was waiting for him when he got home from the hospital … Yes, quite sure, sir. I saw her come out of the flat … Er – no, I didn't pick her up, sir … Well, I started tailing her – and then she took a cab. I followed the cab and – she wasn't in it, sir ... Sorry sir.

CUT TO: Interior of FENTON's flat.

GEORGE: (*Thoughtful; not listening*) Yes, all right, Wall. Thanks for ringing.

(*GEORGE replaces the receiver; he looks angry. He turns towards the bedroom door*)

78

GEORGE: (*Calling*) Mark!

FENTON: (*Calling from the bedroom*) I'll be with you in a minute, George. Help yourself to another drink.

(*A pause. FENTON comes out of the bedroom. He has changed into a lounge suit and a soft shirt*)

FENTON: (*Arranging his tie*) You were just going to tell me about the railway ticket, George.

(*GEORGE faces FENTON; holds his gaze*)

GEORGE: Was I?

FENTON: (*Slightly puzzled*) Yes …

GEORGE: (*A suggestion of contempt*) Don't you know about the ticket?

FENTON: (*Puzzled*) You know perfectly well that I …

(*He stops, looks at the telephone, and then back at GEORGE*)

FENTON: What's happened?

(*GEORGE rises, picks up his hat, crosses to FENTON*)

GEORGE: (*Extremely angry*) You stupid fool, to let a girl incriminate you like this!

FENTON: George, what is it? What's happened?

GEORGE: One of my men tailed you from the hospital.

FENTON: Well?

GEORGE: He was outside when the girl left here.

FENTON: Which girl?

GEORGE: (*In despair*) Oh, Mark …

FENTON: (*Angry*) Which girl? What are you talking about?

GEORGE: (*Turning away from him*) Della Freeman was here when you got back from the hospital. You know perfectly well that she was here …

FENTON: George, I swear to you …

GEORGE: (*Not listening to Fenton, dejected*) You'd better come down to the Yard tomorrow morning. Be there by eleven.

FENTON: George, I swear to you that I haven't seen Della Freeman – not since yesterday!

GEORGE: (*Going out*) Don't be late if you can help it.

(*GEORGE goes out. FENTON stands, staring after him, confused and bewildered. The front door bangs. FENTON turns and crosses to the drinks table; his bewilderment slowly turning to anger and resentment. The telephone starts to ring. FENTON ignores the phone and mixes himself a drink. Suddenly, exasperated, he puts the drink down and crosses to the phone. Lifts receiver.*)

FENTON: (*On phone*) Hello? ... Yes, speaking ... Jackie? Oh, Miss Leroy ... Well, what is it? ... Well, I'm sorry, there's nothing I can do about it. You'll have to ring the hospital tomorrow morning ... (*Irritated*) No, I'm sorry, I can't ...

(*FENTON is about to replace the receiver, then hesitates; he is thinking about what CRAIG said about JACKIE LEROY*)

FENTON: (*Suddenly*) What did you say your address was? ... 14, Pelham Street ... the ground floor flat ... (*After a moment's hesitation*) ... Yes, all right. I'll come round straight away.

(*FENTON replaces the receiver; he looks thoughtful*)

CUT TO: The interior lounge of JACKIE's flat in Earl's Court is a large, faintly exotic room. Ornate cocktail cabinet; shaded lamps; large divan with cushions. There is a door leading to the kitchen and a second door leading to the main bedroom.

JACKIE is reclining on the divan. FENTON is standing by a table, near the divan. There is a large, almost empty box of chocolates on the table. FENTON looks down at JACKIE and smiles.

FENTON: Well, there's absolutely nothing the matter with you at the moment.

JACKIE: But I came over ever so queer, I did really, doctor! Everything went sort of muzzy – it was most peculiar! A sort of blackout it was. I thought I was going to be sick.

(*FENTON picks a chocolate out of the box*)

FENTON: How many of these have you eaten?

JACKIE: Well –

FENTON: Did you open this box to-night?

JACKIE: (*Amused*) Why, of course, silly! It's only a two pound box!

(*FENTON bites the chocolate in half and looks at the inside*)

FENTON: You had a bilious attack, Miss Leroy – and it's not surprising.

(*JACKIE gets up off the divan*)

JACKIE: Well, I feel ever so much better now! I must say, you have quite a way with you, doctor. Let me get you a drink. What would you like, duckie?

FENTON: (*Without hesitation*) A large whisky.

JACKIE: You know what you want, don't you?

(*JACKIE takes a new bottle of whisky from the cupboard in the cabinet, and proceeds to open the bottle*)

FENTON: Miss Leroy, after you left the hospital this afternoon, Dr Craig said rather a curious thing. I've been thinking about it ever since.

JACKIE: (*Turning; bottle in hand*) What did he say?

FENTON: He said, if he was in trouble, serious trouble – with the police for instance – he'd consult you. He said you know exactly what goes on in this town and what you don't know you very soon find out.

(*JACKIE pours the whisky into a glass*)

JACKIE: Did he? I wonder whatever made him say that, now?

FENTON: He must have had a reason?

JACKIE: Yes, I suppose he must. (*Holds up glass*) Do you want water with this or soda?

FENTON: Just as it is, please.

81

JACKIE: (*Taking the drink across to him*) Are you in trouble, Dr Fenton?

FENTON: (*Nodding*) Yes.

JACKIE: What sort of trouble?

FENTON: I'm not sure, but I think the police suspect that I murdered a man.

JACKIE: Really?

(*FENTON nods*)

JACKIE: A patient?

FENTON: Yes.

JACKIE: Oh, dear!

FENTON: No, I don't think you understand. He was a patient of mine that's not why I …

JACKIE: That's not why you murdered him?

FENTON: Yes. (*Quickly*) No! No, that's not what I mean.

JACKIE: It's all right, duckie! I know what you mean all right! Well, what would you like me to do?

(*FENTON takes a drink*)

FENTON: I don't know whether you can do anything, but I was wondering if, by any chance …

(*He puts his glass down on the table near the divan and takes a pencil and a piece of paper out of his pocket*)

FENTON: Look – have you ever seen anything like this before?

(*He draws a Broken Horseshoe on the paper*)

JACKIE: What is it?

(*FENTON shows his drawing to JACKIE*)

FENTON: A broken horseshoe.

JACKIE: (*Tensely*) A broken horseshoe? (*She nods*) Yes …

FENTON: When did you see it?

(*JACKIE looks tense; a little 'on edge'*)

JACKIE: Oh – a few days ago.

FENTON: Where?

JACKIE: (*Turning away from him*) I – I can't remember where.

FENTON: Look, Miss Leroy, only this afternoon you said that if you could do me a favour …

JACKIE: (*Interrupting him*) I've told you, I can't remember where I saw it!

FENTON: But you must remember otherwise you wouldn't have … (*Realises that he is not getting anywhere*) All right, forget it. (*Looks at her; watching*) But tell me one thing – do you know anything about a man called Constance?

JACKIE: Is that the man you're supposed to have murdered?

FENTON: Yes.

JACKIE: (*With a shrug*) The name doesn't mean anything to me. Constance, did you say? Sounds more like a girl, doesn't it? (*Suddenly; 'her old self' again*) Look, duckie, pop into the kitchen and get me a syphon of soda. (*Nods towards the kitchen door*) You'll see it on the table. I'm ever so thirsty. Must be those chocs.

(*FENTON looks at her for a moment and then crosses to the kitchen. There is a look of astonishment on his face. FELIX GALLEGOS is sitting in an armchair, facing FENTON, smiling; revolver in hand*)

GALLEGOS: Good evening, Mr Fenton. How nice to see you again!

END OF PART THREE

Part Four:

MR ERNEST CARREL

OPEN TO: Interior of JACKIE LEROY's flat.
FENTON is facing JACKIE LEROY, watching her.

FENTON: Tell me one thing – do you know anything about a man called Constance?

JACKIE: Is that the man you're supposed to have murdered?

FENTON: Yes.

JACKIE: (*With a shrug*) The name doesn't mean anything to me. Constance, did you say? Sounds more like a girl, doesn't it? (*Suddenly; 'her old self' again*) Look, duckie, pop into the kitchen and get me a syphon of soda. (*Nods towards the kitchen door*) You'll see it on the table. I'm ever so thirsty. Must be those chocs.

(*FENTON looks at her for a moment and then crosses to the kitchen. There is a look of astonishment on his face. FELIX GALLEGOS is sitting in an armchair, facing   FENTON, smiling; revolver in hand*)

GALLEGOS: Good evening, Mr Fenton. How nice to see you again!

FENTON: (*Surprised*) Gallegos!

GALLEGOS: So you remember the name?

FENTON: What are you doing here?

GALLEGOS: I'm the reception committee. A one-man reception committee, for you, Dr Fenton.

FENTON: What is it you want?

GALLEGOS: (*Quietly; angry*) I wanted to return this ticket to you, my friend.

(*He takes the railway ticket out of his waistcoat pocket*)

GALLEGOS: It's not quite what I expected.

(*He tosses the ticket onto the kitchen table*)

FENTON: No?

GALLEGOS: No.

87

(He points to the ticket. FENTON waits a moment and then moves nearer the table and looks down at the ticket.

GALLEGOS stares at FENTON: his hand tightens on the revolver. He is about to shoot)

FENTON:　　　(*Not looking up*) I wouldn't do that, Gallegos.

GALLEGOS:　No?

FENTON:　　　(*Looking at GALLEGOS; shaking his head*) Not if you still want the ticket that Charles Constance gave me.

GALLEGOS:　It's no use bluffing. You haven't got it, my friend. You handed it over to the police.

FENTON:　　　Why do you say that?

GALLEGOS:　You saw Inspector Bellamy.

FENTON:　　　Of course I saw Inspector Bellamy. He's my brother-in-law. I frequently see him; but that doesn't mean I gave him the ticket.

GALLEGOS:　You gave him the ticket all right. You made a fool out of me! (*Raises the revolver*) Now you're going to pay the price.

FENTON:　　　On the contrary, it's you that's going to pay the price.

GALLEGOS:　What do you mean?

FENTON:　　　(*Pointing at the revolver*) If you press that trigger I shall be dead. But I shall still have made a fool out of you. (*Smiling*) You see, Gallegos, it's quite unimportant whether you think I'm bluffing or not. The fact remains, I've got the ticket. (*Leaning forward towards GALLEGOS*) I now know precisely what it's worth.

(GALLEGOS watches FENTON; he is uncertain of him)

GALLEGOS:　I don't believe you.

FENTON:　　　(*With a shrug*) All right. (*Straightens up*) I'm going back into the lounge. If you think I'm bluffing – pull the trigger. But if you do, you'll not only kill me, you'll kill your last chance of getting that railway ticket. Unless of course you don't think it's worth … (*With a smile*) … fifteen   hundred pounds.

(*FENTON turns his back on GALLEGOS and walks out of the kitchen. He looks worried; uncertain of what GALLEGOS will do. We can see GALLEGOS over FENTON's shoulder. He raises the revolver, as if to shoot FENTON in the back, then suddenly changes his mind. FENTON enters the lounge, followed by GALLEGOS. JACKIE is standing by the table, watching GALLEGOS. She is obviously puzzled and a little frightened*)

JACKIE: (*To GALLEGOS*) What's happening?

GALLEGOS: Keep out of this – and keep quiet!

JACKIE: I don't like it! You didn't say there was going to be any rough stuff, you said …

GALLEGOS: Shut up!

JACKIE: (*To FENTON*) I didn't know this was going to happen, doctor – honestly, I didn't. He said it was just a joke.

GALLEGOS: (*Angry; pointing the revolver towards her*) You heard what I said! Keep out of this!

JACKIE: Now look here, this is my flat and I'm not having any hanky-panky! I'm not above earning a pound or two, but really, when it comes to this sort of thing … (*Nods towards the revolver*)

GALLEGOS: I think you'd better go into the kitchen, before I lose my temper.

JACKIE: Well, really!

FENTON: (*Interrupting her*) As your medical adviser, Miss Leroy … (*Looks at GALLEGOS and*

89

<table>
<tr><td></td><td>then across at JACKIE) … I think the kitchen might be a very good idea.</td></tr>
<tr><td>JACKIE:</td><td>(Hesitates) Well – all right! If you say so, doctor.</td></tr>
</table>

(She gives GALLEGOS a 'dirty' look and goes. GALLEGOS turns and, with the revolver pointing at FENTON, locks the kitchen door)

<table>
<tr><td>GALLEGOS:</td><td>Now, Dr Fenton, what makes you think that railway ticket is worth fifteen hundred pounds?</td></tr>
<tr><td>FENTON:</td><td>The fact that you haven't shot me.</td></tr>
<tr><td>GALLEGOS:</td><td>Don't worry, there's plenty of time for that – if it becomes really necessary. (Nods towards settee) Sit down.</td></tr>
</table>

(FENTON sits. GALLEGOS perches himself on the arm of a chair, facing FENTON and next to the drinks table)

GALLEGOS: I want to talk to you.

(He takes a cigarette from the box on the table; flicks his lighter. A pause)

<table>
<tr><td>GALLEGOS:</td><td>You seem to me to be rather a curious young man. I can't quite make up my mind about you.</td></tr>
<tr><td>FENTON:</td><td>Do you mean you can't quite make up your mind whether I've got the ticket or not?</td></tr>
<tr><td>GALLEGOS:</td><td>No, it's not just a question of the ticket. I think you have it all right. (Smiles) But, just at the moment, it's you I'm interested in – not the ticket.</td></tr>
<tr><td>FENTON:</td><td>Is this another attempt to blackmail me?</td></tr>
<tr><td>GALLEGOS:</td><td>No, no, no! It's nothing like that. (Watching FENTON; smoking his cigarette) You've heard of the Broken Horseshoe?</td></tr>
<tr><td>FENTON:</td><td>Yes.</td></tr>
<tr><td>GALLEGOS:</td><td>You know what it is?</td></tr>
</table>

FENTON: (*Hesitating*) Yes, I think so.

GALLEGOS: Does your friend, Inspector Bellamy, know?

FENTON: I haven't discussed it with him.

GALLEGOS: No? What have you discussed with him – our interview at Pinelio's?

(*FENTON shakes his head*)

GALLEGOS: Why not?

FENTON: Because I knew that sooner or later we should meet again and when we did I wanted to make you a proposition.

GALLEGOS: What sort of proposition?

FENTON: I've told you. Fifteen hundred pounds for the railway ticket.

GALLEGOS: (*Smiling*) Are you in need of fifteen hundred pounds?

FENTON: Yes, I am – desperately.

GALLEGOS: (*Amused*) You fellows are all alike. I'll give you seven hundred and fifty …

FENTON: (*Shaking his head*) You'll give me fifteen hundred pounds and you'll agree to certain conditions, otherwise …

GALLEGOS: (*Angry*) Otherwise, what?

FENTON: (*Quite simply*) Otherwise you don't get the ticket.

(*A moment, during which GALLEGOS watches FENTON through a haze of tobacco smoke*)

GALLEGOS: What are the conditions?

FENTON: I want the money in cash – in one pound notes.

GALLEGOS: (*Amused*) Agreed.

FENTON: It's to be handed over to me on Tuesday, mid-day …

GALLEGOS: (*Nodding*) Agreed.

FENTON: … And it's to be handed over by Miss Freeman, with no-one else present. No-one else present, Gallegos.

GALLEGOS: Why Della Freeman?

FENTON: Because there are one or two questions I want to ask her before it's too late.

GALLEGOS: Ask me, doctor. I know the answers.

FENTON: I'm sure you do – but it's not quite the same thing. Well, what do you say?

GALLEGOS: What about the ticket?

FENTON: I'll give it to Miss Freeman when she hands over the money.

GALLEGOS: How do I know it isn't going to be just another ordinary railway ticket?

FENTON: You don't. You've got to take that chance.

(*There is a pause, then GALLEGOS rises*)

GALLEGOS: All right. We'll contact you at the hospital, probably some time tomorrow afternoon. (*He stands by the table; faces FENTON*) But, don't try any funny business, doctor. (*Looks at the revolver he is holding*) Because, if you do, next time I shan't even listen to what you've got to say. (*Smiling; picks up a bottle from the table*) Now, let me mix you a drink …

FENTON: (*Rising*) No, thank you. You mixed me a drink once before, remember …

GALLEGOS: Oh, yes! Yes … (*He is amused; starts to laugh*) I like you – you have a sense of humour. (*He goes to the cocktail cabinet – pours himself a drink*) Salut! (*He drinks the drink down in one*) Give my love to Jackie. (*He leaves the flat*)

92

(*FENTON quickly unlocks the kitchen door and JACKIE re-enters. She is in obvious pain with her wrist which she has attempted to bandage*)

JACKIE: Has he gone?

FENTON: Yes. Does your wrist hurt you?

JACKIE: (*In obvious pain*) Yes, it does.

(*JACKIE crosses towards the settee*)

FENTON: You seem to have some very nice friends, Miss Leroy.

JACKIE: (*Angry*) He's no friend of mine.

FENTON: Well, I hope you didn't invite him here for my benefit.

JACKIE: I didn't invite him at all, he … (*She winces in pain*)

(*FENTON quietly; taking her wrist and examines it*)

FENTON: Does that hurt you? Let me have a look.

JACKIE: (*Hesitant*) no.

FENTON: Move it slightly – does it hurt?

(*JACKIE twists her wrist and suddenly winces with pain. FENTON unties the bandage and takes it off JACKIE's wrist*)

FENTON: I'll put this bandage back on for you. If it isn't any better by tomorrow morning, drop into the hospital and see Dr Craig.

JACKIE: What, Scottie! I wouldn't trust him with a sore finger.

FENTON: He may be Scottie to you, Miss Leroy, but to us he's Mortimer Charles Duncan Craig, M.B.C.H.B.

JACKIE: Mortimer! He doesn't look like a Mortimer!

FENTON: (*Watching her*) Appearances are frequently deceptive – you don't look like a friend of Gallegos'.

JACKIE: (*Tensely*) I've told you I'm not a friend of his.

FENTON: Then what was he doing here?

JACKIE: (*Hesitant*) He found out that I knew you and he asked me to invite you here. He said he just wanted to have a little chat.

FENTON: I see.

JACKIE: (*Watching him*) You don't believe me, do you?

FENTON: No, I'm afraid I don't. I've got a shrewd suspicion you know all about Felix Gallegos – all about the Broken Horseshoe.

JACKIE: I don't know what you're talking about! Really, I've never heard such nonsense!

FENTON: I thought you were a friend of mine, Jackie?

JACKIE: I am. But you're not the only pebble on the beach. Besides I've got to watch my step. I don't want to get mixed up in any funny business. It wouldn't be good for my – (*She changes her mind*) for me.

FENTON: Jackie, have you ever heard of a girl called Della Freeman?

JACKIE: No – no, I haven't.

FENTON: Do you know why Gallegos wanted the railway ticket?

JACKIE: No, I don't. Look, Mr Fenton, it's no good you asking me a lot of questions, because I just don't know the answers. Honest, duckie, I just don't know the answers.

(*A pause. FENTON looks at her*)

FENTON: You know the answers all right, Jackie. Give me your wrist.

(*FENTON starts to bandage her wrist*)

CUT TO: Car park at Scotland Yard.
A police car drives into the quadrangle. GEORGE gets out of it and enters the main building.

CUT TO: SUPERINTENDENT GRAYSON's office at Scotland Yard is a large comfortable room: desk, armchairs, map on the wall of Metropolitan areas. Photographs of police events, social and sporting.

SUPERINTENDENT GRAYSON is sitting behind the desk, finishing a letter. LONG, a uniformed clerk, stands by the side of the desk. He is holding a manilla folder containing photographs of Charles Constance. There is a knock on the door.

GRAYSON: Come in!

(*GEORGE enters*)

GEORGE: Good morning, sir!

GRAYSON: Oh, hello, Bellamy.

(*GEORGE crosses towards the desk and sits on the arm of one of the armchairs. GRAYSON finishes the letter, puts it in an envelope, licks down the flap of the envelope, and hands it to Long*)

GRAYSON: (*To GEORGE*) What time are we expecting that brother-in-law of yours?

GEORGE: I said eleven o'clock, sir.

GRAYSON: Oh good. (*To Long*) I want you to take this to Chief-Inspector Howard – don't give it to anyone else.

LONG: Yes, sir.

GRAYSON: (*Pointing at the folder*) What's that you've got?

LONG: The Constance photographs, sir. You asked for them.

GRAYSON: Oh, yes. Of course. (*Takes folder from Long*) All right, Long.

LONG: Thank you, sir.

(*LONG goes out. GRAYSON yawns; stretches himself; suddenly winces*)

GRAYSON: (*Irritable*) This fibrositis of mine seems to be getting worse.

95

GEORGE: I'm sorry.

GRAYSON: I feel like a piece of chewed string this morning. (*Takes a document off the desk*) I've been reading that statement again – the one your brother-in-law made.

GEORGE: Yes?

GRAYSON: You know, I think he's telling the truth. I even think he was telling the truth about that girl.

GEORGE: I wish I could think so, sir. (*Shakes his head*) No, she went to the flat all right. West saw her come out.

GRAYSON: West may have seen her come out – I don't doubt that he did – but that doesn't mean that Fenton had an appointment with her. It doesn't necessarily mean that he even saw the girl.

GEORGE: But he must have seen her.

GRAYSON: I'm not so sure. If Fenton had had an appointment with her, he'd have given her the key and told her to let herself into the flat.

GEORGE: But that's precisely what happened! She did let herself into the flat.

GRAYSON: Yes, but not with Fenton's key.

GEORGE: How do you know?

(*GRAYSON rises and moves round to the front of the desk; he moves his arms as he walks, a deliberate movement, trying to ease his fibrositis*)

GRAYSON: I wasn't satisfied with that explanation of yours, so I sent Sergeant North down to take a look at the lock. It had obviously been tampered with. The girl got into the flat without Fenton knowing anything about it.

GEORGE: But he must have seen her, sir, otherwise …
              (*He hesitates*)
GRAYSON: Well?
GEORGE: (*Thoughtfully*) I was just thinking. Mark took
              a bath. If he went straight into the bedroom as
                    soon as he arrived it is possible … I
              wonder if that's what happened?
GRAYSON: Well, it's a theory anyway. I think you've got
              to consider it even if you don't give him the
              benefit of the doubt.
GEORGE: (*His thoughts elsewhere*) Yes …
GRAYSON: How long have you known Fenton?
GEORGE: Oh, I should say about fifteen years. I've been
              married nearly twelve.
GRAYSON: Before this business happened, would you
              have trusted him?
GEORGE: Good Lord, yes! Implicitly.
GRAYSON: (*Nods*) Well, there you are, you see. You
              know, Bellamy, it's my experience that
              people don't change overnight. You were
              either wrong about Fenton in the first place or
              you're wrong about him now! We'll see what
              he's got to say for himself anyway.
(*There is a knock on the door*)
GRAYSON: Come in.
(*LONG enters*)
LONG: Excuse me, sir.
GRAYSON: Yes?
LONG: Mr Carrel's here, sir.
GRAYSON: (*Nodding*) Send him up.
LONG: Yes, sir.
(*LONG goes*)
GEORGE: Is that Ernest Carrel?

97

GRAYSON: Yes. I sent for him. (*He turns towards the photographs on his desk*) I want him to take a look at these photographs.

GEORGE: Of Mr Constance?

GRAYSON: Yes.

GEORGE: Another theory, Superintendent?

GRAYSON: M'm – m'm. (*Works his shoulder blades*) I'm full of 'em this morning. Theories and fibrositis!

(*GEORGE laughs, returns to the armchair*)

GEORGE: What sort of a bird is Ernest Carrel? I've read a lot about him.

GRAYSON: He's rather a curious mixture. When you first meet him you think he's typically English. You know, the out-door type. Horses, dogs, eighteen holes on a Sunday morning. But after a while you begin to wonder. You notice his clothes are just a little too well cut, his fancy waistcoats perhaps a shade too fancy.

GEORGE: Is he as rich as they say he is?

GRAYSON: Well, when Mrs Van Delson died he inherited three quarters of a million – quite apart from her string of race-horses.

GEORGE: Is that how he started in the race game?

GRAYSON: Yes. He wasn't worth a bob until he met Mrs Van Delson. (*Laughing*) And do you know where they met?

(*GEORGE shakes his head*)

GRAYSON: Bournemouth – in August.

GEORGE: And they say it's relaxing! Was she older than Carrel?

GRAYSON: Considerably older. She was seventy odd when she died.

GEORGE: When was that?

(*There is a knock on the door*)

GRAYSON: (*Turning towards the door*) About two years ago. Come in.

(*LONG enters*)

LONG: Mr Carrel, sir.

(*ERNEST CARREL enters. He is in his early thirties; his dress and manner is just a little 'larger than life'. LONG leaves*)

GRAYSON: Come in, Mr Carrel. (*Introducing GEORGE*) Inspector Bellamy.

CARREL: How d'ye do, Inspector.

GRAYSON: (*Indicating the armchair*) Sit down, Mr Carrel.

CARREL: (*Crossing to the chair and sitting*) Thank you. (*He takes off his gloves*) What an extraordinary day. When I got up this morning I thought it was going to be perfectly lovely.

GRAYSON: I'm sorry to have to drag you up to town.

CARREL: Not at all. As a matter of fact I was coming up this afternoon anyway. I'm staying at the Ritz for two or three weeks.

(*GRAYSON picks up the box of cigarettes on his desk and offers it to Carrel*)

GRAYSON: Cigarette?

CARREL: (*Taking out his case*) If you don't mind I'd prefer one of my own. (*Offers case to GEORGE*) Inspector?

GEORGE: No, thank you.

(*CARREL offers the case to GRAYSON but the Superintendent shakes his head. CARREL takes out a lighter and lights a cigarette*)

GRAYSON: I had another talk to Lord Wexley yesterday afternoon. It appears the Stewards are still very concerned about 'Siesta'.

99

CARREL: So am I, Superintendent – very concerned.
             But what can one do about it? Incidentally,
             while I'm here there's a point I'd like to
             mention. (*Smiling*) Just in case you, or Lord
             Wexley, or the Stewards of the Jockey Club,
             are under any misapprehension.

GRAYSON: Yes?

CARREL: My horse may have been doped – although
             quite frankly I don't think it was – but the
             point I'd like to make clear – perfectly clear –
             is that I backed a horse called 'Soft Velvet'. It
             came fifth. I lost precisely eight hundred and
             fifty pounds.

GRAYSON: (*With deliberate charm*) My dear Mr Carrel,
             no-one is suggesting – least of all Lord
             Wexley or the Jockey Club – that you had
             anything to do with the doping of the horse.

CARREL: And Scotland Yard?

GRAYSON: (*Smiling*) So far as Scotland Yard are
             concerned we never suggest anything – we
             just investigate.

GEORGE: Incidentally, you may not have won anything
             on 'Siesta' – but I did! I won six pounds ten
             shillings and was highly delighted.

(*They all laugh*)

GRAYSON: I'm going to be frank with you, Mr Carrel.
             This business has a slightly … (*Searching for
             words*) … wider implication, otherwise we
             shouldn't be so concerned.

CARREL: (*Faintly irritated*) What do you mean – a
             wider implication? Isn't that a little
             ambiguous?

GEORGE: The Superintendent means that, in our opinion, it isn't just a question of doping a horse. It goes much deeper than that.

CARREL: Indeed?

(*GEORGE looks at GRAYSON who nods his head*)

GEORGE: It's a question of – murder.

CARREL: Murder!

GRAYSON: Yes. Mr Carrel, have you heard of a group of people – a gang if you like – who call themselves the Broken Horseshoe?

CARREL: (*Hesitating*) Why, no …

GRAYSON: Well, the Broken Horseshoe gang specialises in doping horses. It's our opinion they were responsible for 'Wedgewood' in the Evening Stakes, 'Pinpoint' at Aintree, and 'Siesta'.

CARREL: But surely, if you know these people why don't you arrest them?

GRAYSON: Unfortunately, it's not quite so simple as that. (*Holding out the photographs*) Mr Carrel, I want you to take a look at these photographs – and tell me whether you've seen this man before.

CARREL: (*Taking photographs*) Who is it?

GRAYSON: Take a look. Perhaps you can tell me.

(*GRAYSON and GEORGE watch CARREL as he studies the photographs. There is a flicker of recognition in Carrel's expression, but he quickly conceals it. GEORGE glances across at GRAYSON*)

GRAYSON: Well?

CARREL: (*Calmly; shaking his head*) No, I've never seen him before.

GRAYSON: You're sure?

(*GRAYSON takes the photographs from CARREL and turns towards the desk*)

CARREL: Perfectly sure. Who is he?

GRAYSON: His name's Constance. He was knocked down
             on the Brompton Road and taken to St
             Matthew's Hospital. About a week after he
             left the hospital he was murdered.

CARREL: (*Quietly*) Who murdered him?

GRAYSON: (*Looking straight at Carrel*) We don't know,
             Mr Carrel – not yet.

CARREL: Well, I'm afraid I don't quite see what all this
             has got to do with my horse – 'Siesta'.

GRAYSON: Constance was one of the people who knew
             that 'Siesta' was going to win. He tipped it a
             fortnight before the race.

CARREL: Quite a lot of people did. After all, the
             Inspector went one better, he backed it!
             (*Rises: amused*) I'm sorry, but I can't
             believe that was just because this   Mr   …
             What was the name?

GRAYSON: Constance.

CARREL: I can't believe that just because Mr Constance
             tipped my horse he was responsible for
             doping it. Always providing of course, that it
             was doped.

(*GRAYSON taps the photographs on the desk: drawing
attention to them*)

GRAYSON: Anyway, you've never seen him?

(*CARREL moves to the side of the desk*)

CARREL: (*Pleasantly*) Never. I'd never even heard of
             the gentleman until you mentioned his name.

CARREL: No. (*Looking down at the photographs*) He's
             got rather distinctive features hasn't he? I
             don't think I should forget a face like that.

(*GRAYSON holds out his hand; dismissing CARREL*)

GRAYSON: No, I'm sure you wouldn't. I'm sorry to have troubled you.

(*CARREL shakes hands with GRAYSON and moves towards the door*)

CARREL: No trouble at all. (*To GEORGE*) Goodbye, Inspector.

GEORGE: Goodbye.

(*GRAYSON takes CARREL to the door. GEORGE watches as CARREL exits. The door closes and GRAYSON returns to GEORGE*)

GEORGE: (*Quietly; serious*) He recognised the photographs.

GRAYSON: (*Thoughtful*) Yes.

GEORGE: Do you think he knew Constance, or do you think he'd just seen him somewhere?

(*GRAYSON moves his shoulders; the fibrositis is troubling him again*)

GRAYSON: It's my bet he knew him. I've a hunch that Constance has something on Carrel and blackmailed him into doping the horse.

(*There is a knock on the door and LONG enters*)

GRAYSON: Yes?

LONG: Mr Fenton's here, sir.

GRAYSON: Fetch him in, please.

LONG: Yes, sir.

(*LONG goes. The telephone stars to ring. GRAYSON crosses to the desk and lifts the receiver*)

GRAYSON: (*On phone*) Hello? … Speaking … Oh, hello, Briggs … Yes? … Yes …Good … I'll be down in about half an hour. (*Replaces the receiver: to GEORGE*) That was the Lab – they've got a report on the railway ticket.

GEORGE: Oh, good!

GRAYSON: (*Hesitatingly*) Bellamy, I think it might be quite a good idea if I saw Fenton on his own.

GEORGE: (*Considering the suggestion*) Yes, of course sir, I'll go down to the Lab.

(*GEORGE crosses to the door as LONG opens it and FENTON appears*)

GEORGE: Come in, Mark!

(*FENTON enters; he looks worried; a shade apprehensive about the forthcoming interview*)

FENTON: Hello, George!

GEORGE: (*To GRAYSON*) This is my brother-in-law, sir.

GRAYSON: How-do-you-do, Mr Fenton?

(*FENTON nods and shakes hands with GRAYSON*)

GEORGE: (*To FENTON: on his way out*) I'll probably see you later.

FENTON: (*Nodding*) Yes, all right.

(*GEORGE leaves*)

GRAYSON: Sit down, Mr Fenton.

CUT TO: Police Laboratory.

GEORGE and WALTER BRIGGS are standing by a sink which has a flat draining board; there are various photographic materials, enlarger, microscope, etc ... by the side of the sink. In the sink itself there is a dish containing a coloured liquid and an enlarged photograph of the railway ticket. BRIGGS is holding the actual ticket in his hand. WALTER BRIGGS is a clever, rather self-satisfied man. He wears a white coat.

BRIGGS: My word, we've had quite a game with this ticket, Inspector.

GEORGE: Yes, I expect you have.

BRIGGS: Frankly, at one time, I thought we were going to draw a blank.

(*GEORGE is determined to "rub" BRIGGS up the right way*)

GEORGE: I don't know how you boys do it. I just wouldn't know where to start. (*Smiles at BRIGGS*) But don't tell the Superintendent that.

BRIGGS: (*Rather pleased with himself*) Well, when you're dealing with secret handwriting, the first thing you've got to find out is what particular substance they've used; having found that you've got to find the right developer. That isn't always easy.

GEORGE: I'll bet it isn't.

BRIGGS: (*Looking at the railway ticket*) We had a devil of a game with this little fellow. You'd be surprised! Ultra-violet light, silver nitrate, the whole bag of tricks.

GEORGE: Anyway, you did it.

BRIGGS: Oh, we did it all right. We don't let many things beat us. Not if we can help it.

(*He picks up the photograph out of the dish*)

BRIGGS: Once we'd revealed the handwriting, I had the ticket photographed.

(*He hands the photograph to GEORGE*)

GEORGE: (*Taking photograph*) Good!

BRIGGS: (*Pointing*) You see the writing?

GEORGE: (*Thoughtfully*) Yes. (*Reading*) 'Ernest Carrel alias Merton Smith alias Carl Brunner. Zurich, May '45. Lisbon, June '46.

BRIGGS: (*Smiling*) Don't ask me what it means – that's your pigeon.

GEORGE: (*Quietly*) Yes. (*He looks very thoughtful*) Carl Brunner …?

CUT TO: *A UNIFORMED POLICE CLERK is searching through a large file in a corner of the Records Department at Scotland Yard. GEORGE stands by his side watching him.*

CLERK: (*Looking up*) We've got nearly three thousand Smiths, sir – and a hundred and eighty-nine Brunners.

GEORGE: (*Briskly*) Right! Cross-check with the Zurich and Lisbon files. Zurich, May '45. Lisbon, June '46.

CLERK: Yes, sir!

(*The CLERK looks through a file and takes out some cards which he hands to GEORGE*)

CLERK: I think this is what you want, sir.

(*GEORGE studies the cards; he looks very pleased*)

GEORGE: (*Delighted*) This is it! Thanks.

CUT TO: Interior of GRAYSON's office.

GRAYSON is standing by the desk, speaking on the telephone.

GRAYSON: … Yes, get the description out straight away … Felix Poling, alias Gallegos …

(*GEORGE enters during GRAYSON's conversation. He is carrying a sheaf of papers and the cards handed to him by the POLICE CLERK*)

GRAYSON: … Yes … (*Irritated*) Yes, of course, particularly in the London area. Right! (*He replaces the receiver and moves round to the front of the desk*) Did you see Fenton?

GEORGE: No.

GRAYSON: He's only just this minute left. (*Leans against the desk*) I like that brother-in-law of yours.

GEORGE: I like him, sir, only I can't make up my mind whether he's telling the truth.

GRAYSON: I think he is. He fell for that girl. Of course she obviously played him up; but I think he's

got wise to it. By the way, you know that
fellow Gallegos he was telling you about?

GEORGE: Yes?

GRAYSON: It's our old friend Poling.

GEORGE: Well, I'm blowed!

GRAYSON: We went through the gallery together and
Fenton spotted him in one of the Paris
photographs.

GEORGE: What about the girl?

GRAYSON: We can't place her – not yet, but we will.
Anyway, there's one interesting piece of
information. They still think Fenton's got the
ticket. (*Suddenly*) Oh, by the way, what did
Briggs have to say?

(*GEORGE hands GRAYSON one of the documents he is
carrying*)

GEORGE: The actual railway ticket was a blind – a rather
clever one, though, I must confess.

GRAYSON: What do you mean – there was a message on
it?

(*GEORGE nods*)

GRAYSON: What was it?

GEORGE: (*Nodding at the paper GRAYSON is holding*)
I've made a copy of it, sir.

GRAYSON: (*Looking at the paper*) M'm …

GEORGE: You were obviously right about Constance –
he was blackmailing Carrel.

GRAYSON: Yes – he looks like it. (*Looks up at GEORGE*)
Have you checked this?

GEORGE: Yes, Mr Ernest Carrel, alias Morton Smith,
alias Carl Brunner, seems to have quite a
history. (*He passes GRAYSON the rest of the
papers*) Makes interesting reading …

(*GRAYSON looks at the documents thoughtfully*)

107

CUT TO: *FENTON is sitting at the desk in his office. He is writing a report in a journal. DR DUNCAN CRAIG enters; he is boisterously agitated.*

CRAIG: Fenton, for goodness sake give me a cigarette!

FENTON: (*Looking up*) Mr Armitage?

CRAIG: Mr Armitage! I've told Sister Rogers, I've told Gillespie, if they don't get that man transferred to another ward I shall go stark staring mad!

FENTON: (*Throwing a box of matches to him*) You don't want him in another ward, old boy – you want him in another hospital.

CRAIG: I just don't understand it! The man's fantastic! He's suffering from (*fill in medical term*) and (*fill in medical term*) and last night he smoked two cigars and drank half a bottle of Scotch.

FENTON: (*Laughing*) But where does he get the stuff?

CRAIG: (*Shaking his head*) I don't know. We watch him like a hawk, but it's no use – it's not a bit of use. Frankly, it's getting to the stage where I wouldn't be surprised to pop upstairs and find his wife in bed with him. What do you think would happen if I murdered Mr Armitage?

FENTON: He'd die.

CRAIG: Yes, I know that, but what do you think would happen to me?

FENTON: They'd probably make you R.S.O. at St Julian's.

CRAIG: (*Laughing*) Heaven forbid! Are you off duty tonight?

FENTON: I'm not sure yet.

(*CRAIG stubs out his cigarette; sits on a corner of the desk, looking down at FENTON*)

CRAIG: Fenton, there's something I'd rather like to ask you. I hope you won't take offence.

FENTON: Why should I?

CRAIG: Well, it's rather personal.

FENTON: Most things are.

CRAIG: Well, the fact of the matter is – (*Looks down at his hands*) I'm broke.

FENTON: Broke?

CRAIG: That's right. (*Looks up; smiles*) I haven't got any money.

FENTON: But you must have some?

CRAIG: Oh, I've got some, of course. (*Gets off the desk, takes coins out of his pocket and looks at them*) Eight and six.

FENTON: You mean to say that's all the money you've got in the world?

CRAIG: I'm afraid so. As a matter of fact, this isn't really my eight and six.

FENTON: Well, whose is it?

CRAIG: Well, you see, two weeks ago I borrowed thirty pounds from somebody and I haven't paid them back, so I suppose, strictly speaking this is their eight and six.

FENTON: (*Faintly bewildered*) Yes, I suppose it is. (*Looks up*) Who did you borrow the money from?

CRAIG: (*Vaguely*) Oh, just a friend of mine.

FENTON: Not a patient?

(*CRAIG looks embarrassed*)

CRAIG: No, no, he's not a patient – not at the moment.

FENTON: (*Quietly*) Who was it?

CRAIG: Oh, dear, I don't think you're going to like this.

FENTON: Well?

CRAIG: Do you remember that big fellow in ward eight – he left about ten days ago?

109

FENTON: The motor car salesman?

(*CRAIG nods*)

FENTON: Oh, no! No, you couldn't!

CRAIG: I could – I did!

FENTON: But Craig …

CRAIG: I know! I know exactly what you're thinking. But I was in a spot, Fenton! I was in a terrible hole. Besides, he asked for it. Swanking about all the money he made. He was a spiv anyway, that's all he was – a chromium-plated spiv!

(*In spite of the outburst CRAIG is a little ashamed of himself. There is a pause. CRAIG faces FENTON again*)

CRAIG: Sorry.

FENTON: How much do you need?

CRAIG: I need … three hundred …

FENTON: Three hundred!

CRAIG: Yes. I know it's a lot, but – I'm in a mess. I'm really in a first-class hole.

FENTON: But look here, Craig – why the devil should I lend you three hundred pounds?

CRAIG: (*Hesitates; turns away*) I'm sorry, Fenton. I shouldn't have asked you. If you can't afford it then …

FENTON: (*Interrupting him*) It isn't a question of not affording it. I can afford it all right – that's not the point. Was that your car I saw you driving the other day?

CRAIG: No, it belongs to a friend of mine.

FENTON: Why doesn't he lend you the three hundred pounds?

CRAIG: He's – not that sort of a friend.

FENTON: (*Shaking his head*) I'm sorry, Craig, there's nothing I can do about it.

110

CRAIG: All right. I suppose I shall just have to starve. It's been done before. (*Suddenly; a last attempt*) Look, will you lend me two hundred, till the end of June?

FENTON: Why the end of June?

CRAIG: Well, my old man comes across at the end of June and …

FENTON: And supposing your old man doesn't come across?

CRAIG: But he must! Oh … What a horrible thought!

(*FENTON opens a drawer in the desk and takes out his cheque book; picks up his pen*)

FENTON: Look, Craig – I'll let you have a hundred.

(*CRAIG beams: FENTON signs the cheque*)

CRAIG: You're a pal. A real pal!

FENTON: (*Handing CRAIG the cheque*) I'm a first-class chump. And you know it! Give me an IOU and let me have it back by Christmas.

(*CRAIG grins; folds the cheque and puts it in his pocket*)

CRAIG: June, old boy. Definitely June.

(*SISTER ROGERS enters; she carries a letter*)

SISTER: (*Handing the letter to FENTON*) There's a letter for you. It was delivered by hand.

FENTON: (*Rising*) Oh, thanks. (*Opens the letter*)

SISTER: (*To CRAIG*) Dr Gillespie would like to see you, doctor. He's in Ward 6.

CRAIG: I'll be right up.

(*SISTER ROGERS goes. FENTON is staring at a Yale key which he has taken from the envelope: he holds a sheet of notepaper in his hand*)

CRAIG: (*To FENTON*) I'll see you later, Fenton.

FENTON: (*Looking up; his thoughts elsewhere*) M'm? Oh, yes.

CRAIG: And many thanks.

111

FENTON: That's all right.

(*CRAIG smiles at FENTON and leaves. FENTON is reading the note he has received. FENTON turns towards the desk. He picks up the telephone and dials a number. A pause*)

FENTON: Give me an outside line, please. (*He dials a number*) Put me through to Superintendent Grayson, please.

(*Camera pans in on the note FENTON received. It reads:*)

Dear Mr Fenton,

I shall expect you tomorrow evening about six o'clock, at 21 Ellsworth Crescent. I am sending you the key as I may be late.

Della Freeman

CUT TO: A police car is stationed at the corner of a quiet London street.

GEORGE and SUPERINTENDENT GRAYSON are sitting in the car with uniformed officers. FENTON appears, in the distance, and walks down the street. GEORGE looks at GRAYSON and gives a significant nod. FENTON arrives at the front door of one of the houses; he takes out the key, hesitates; looks up and down the street, and then inserts the key in the lock and opens the front door. He enters the house.

CUT TO: The interior of the old-fashioned hall of 21 Ellsworth Court, complete with hat-stand, etc.

FENTON enters the hall through the front door. He closes the door behind him and looks slowly round the hall. He moves across the hall to the drawing room door, hesitates; then opens the door. He enters the drawing room. It is a large old-fashioned room with a large wing chair in the far corner, a heavy Victorian table, a canary in a cage, heavy ornamental side-table, settee, chairs, etc. FENTON takes in the room; realises that DELLA has not yet arrived; looks at his wristlet watch. He crosses to the canary, puts his finger on the cage, and whistles at the bird. He then turns again ... from the canary cage, taking in the various objects: the heavy furniture, ornamental vases, bookcase, china cupboard, wing chair ... Suddenly, and quite without warning, a woman's hand drops limply over the side of the chair. There is a large ring on the third finger. We recognise the ring. It is JACKIE LEROY's.

END OF PART FOUR

Part Five:

MR MARK FENTON

OPEN TO: The drawing room of 21 Ellsworth Crescent. *FENTON touches the dead JACKIE LEROY's hand and then her face.*

CUT TO: Lab at Scotland Yard.
GEORGE is standing by KEITH PHIPPS who is about thirty-five and wears horn-rimmed spectacles. He is examining a slide through a microscope. There is a bullet on a piece of white cloth near the microscope. GEORGE looks impatient.
GEORGE: Well?
PHIPPS: (*Looking up*) It's difficult to say, exactly …
GEORGE: Well, give me a rough idea.
PHIPPS: I don't like giving rough ideas, Inspector. It's my job to be accurate. (*Indicates slide*) I'm trying to find the precise type of powder. When I've done that I shall be in a position to tie it up with the bullet.
GEORGE: Yes, I appreciate that – but how long is it going to take?
(*PHIPPS studies the slide again; removes it, picks up the bullet with a pair of forceps and places it in position for examination*)
PHIPPS: Oh, difficult to say. All depends.
GEORGE: (*With sarcasm*) Of course this could go on all night!
PHIPPS: (*Unmoved*) Yes, it could.
(*The door opens and LONG enters*)
LONG: Excuse me, sir.
GEORGE: Yes?
LONG: Here's the ring you were asking for, sir. Mr Wilson has finished with it.
GEORGE: Thank you.

(*LONG hands the ring to GEORGE then goes out. There is a pause, then PHIPPS suddenly looks up and smiles at GEORGE*)

PHIPPS: If I were you I should look for a revolver, Inspector – Nagant type, though probably not a true Nagant. Four lands, four grooves.

GEORGE: (*Pleased*) Thanks. Now take a look at this. There's some blood on it. We want a grouping.

PHIPPS: Tonight?

GEORGE: Yes – straight away.

PHIPPS: (*Shaking his head; faintly exasperated*) Who was this woman, anyway?

GEORGE: Her name was Jackie Leroy.

CUT TO: SUPERINTENDENT GRAYSON's office. *GRAYSON is sitting on the edge of his desk. FENTON is standing against a large wall map.*

GRAYSON: You've got to face the facts, Fenton. And they're not particularly pleasant.

FENTON: You mean what happened to Jackie Leroy might happen to me?

GRAYSON: (*Nodding*) Yes.

FENTON: Why do you think they murdered Jackie?

GRAYSON: She probably knew too much.

FENTON: I don't think Jackie Leroy was mixed up in this business – I mean really mixed up in it. I don't think she knew about the railway ticket, for instance.

GRAYSON: I'm inclined to agree with you. She had a police record but it didn't include anything of this sort. No, I think they got rid of Jackie for two reasons. First, because she began to get curious …

118

FENTON: (*Nodding*) I saw an example of that …

GRAYSON: … And second because they wanted to scare you.

FENTON: Well, they certainly did that all right!

GRAYSON: But the point that intrigues me is this. You obviously convinced Gallegos that you had the railway ticket, and he obviously thought that you were prepared to sell it for fifteen hundred pounds. (*FENTON nods*) That's why he let you go that night at Jackie Leroy's and why they sent you the key to Ellsworth Crescent.

FENTON: Yes.

GRAYSON: Now something happened after they sent you that key. Someone warned Gallegos – or the girl – that you'd either been double-crossing them all   along.

FENTON: But nothing happened. I received the key and I kept the appointment.

GRAYSON: (*Thoughtfully*) Yes.

(*There is a knock on the door*)

GRAYSON: Come in!

(*GEORGE enters*)

FENTON: Don't you think we've reached the stage where we could be perfectly frank with each other?

GRAYSON: I thought we were being frank.

FENTON: (*Shaking his head*) I'm mixed up in this business. I'm even taking a risk – you've admitted that yourself. (*GRAYSON nods*) But I still don't know what it's all about. I still don't understand why Gallegos should want the railway ticket.

119

GRAYSON:	Sit down both of you. Constance, the man you operated on, was a blackmailer. He discovered certain information about a wealthy racehorse owner called Ernest Carrel. He inscribed this information – in invisible ink – on a railway ticket.
FENTON:	But why on a railway ticket? It seems a bit far-fetched. Why not a piece of notepaper?
GRAYSON:	Because Constance knew perfectly well that if anything happened to him, an ordinary letter or any other sort of document found on him would be carefully scrutinised, but it was a pretty good chance that no one would think of examining an ordinary railway ticket. And if you had posted it as he intended, probably no one would have examined it.
FENTON:	I see. So it isn't really as far-fetched as it appeared.
GRAYSON:	By no means. And the use of invisible ink is much more common than the man in the street imagines. Then he contacted an organisation known as the Broken Horseshoe. He told them he was in a position to blackmail Carrel providing they made it worth his while. (*FENTON nods*) They decided to play in with him, so Constance blackmailed Carrel into allowing the Broken Horseshoe gang to dope 'Siesta'. Well, you know what happened – the horse won.
GEORGE:	And Mr Gallegos and his friends made a packet.
GRAYSON:	Exactly! But Gallegos wasn't satisfied with that, he knew that Constance had this

	information about Carrel and he wanted to get hold of it.
FENTON:	Yes, but I don't see why Constance risked giving me the ticket in the first place?
GRAYSON:	He naturally thought you'd post the letter.
GEORGE:	You see, Constance didn't intend that anyone else should blackmail Carrel. But he'd made up his mind that if anything happened to him the information he possessed should go straight to his girlfriend and not to Gallegos.
FENTON:	I see. So no-one knew what was on the ticket except Constance?
GRAYSON:	No-one.
FENTON:	But who was his girlfriend? The envelope he gave me was addressed to a Mrs Kelsey.
GRAYSON:	(*To GEORGE*) Show him the photograph, Bellamy.
GEORGE:	Yes, sir.

(*GEORGE crosses to the bookcase*)

GRAYSON:	Come over here and look at this.

(*Under the front-face photograph of DELLA FREEMAN is written in handwriting, on negative: "File 7/k389/NICE FILE 4J/ BARBARA MASON"*)

GEORGE:	Is this Della Freeman?
FENTON:	Why, yes!
GEORGE:	(*Nodding, closing the album*) It's also the same person who took the flat at Drayton Court under the name of Kelsey. Her real name by the way is Barbara Mason.
FENTON:	(*Hesitant*) Has she a police record?
GEORGE:	Yes. In France as well …
FENTON:	(*Quietly*) I see.
GEORGE:	I'm sorry, Mark.

121

FENTON: Well, it looks as if I shall have to chalk it up to experience, doesn't it? Do you think she murdered Constance?

GRAYSON: No. I think she double-crossed him and tried to sell him out to Gallegos, but I don't think she murdered him.

FENTON: Then who did? And who put the sign on the mirror?

GRAYSON: (*Sits*) We don't know yet but we have our suspicions.

FENTON: (*Sits*) What was it exactly that Constance discovered – about Ernest Carrel, I mean?

GRAYSON: He discovered that he'd a criminal record and was known in Zurich as Carl Brunner. The Portuguese police knew him as Morton Smith – a so-called publicity expert.

FENTON: I see. Does that mean you're going to arrest Carrel?

GRAYSON: Not yet. We've other fish to fry at the moment.

GEORGE: It's the Broken Horseshoe crowd we're after, Mark. Gallegos, and the girl, whoever else is mixed up in it.

FENTON: Well, I've a hunch I could find Gallegos for you.

GEORGE: How?

FENTON: I think he'll still make an attempt to blackmail Carrel.

GRAYSON: But he can't. Constance didn't tell him anything and he hasn't seen the ticket – the real ticket.

FENTON: Carrell was blackmailed by Constance into allowing Gallegos and his crowd to dope 'Siesta', right?

122

GEORGE: Right.
FENTON: Well, supposing Gallegos threatens Carrel to
             tell about the 'Siesta' affair? Carrel will
             naturally assume that Gallegos knows as
             much about him as Constance did.
GRAYSON: (*Thoughtfully*) Yes, that might well happen …
FENTON: So Carrel might very easily lead you to
             Gallegos.
GRAYSON: Yes, but Carrel won't talk, he'd sooner do
             anything than get mixed up with the police.
FENTON: Don't you think he could be made to talk? At
             least, he could be made to get in touch with
             you if Gallegos contacts him.
GRAYSON: How?
FENTON: Well – I could talk to him, for instance. He
             doesn't know who I am – or whose side I'm
             on.
GRAYSON: But how could you influence Ernest Carrel?
FENTON: Quite simply. (*Smiles*) I could blackmail him.
GRAYSON: Blackmail him!
FENTON: Yes – I know what's on the ticket.
(*GRAYSON looks at GEORGE, obviously intrigued by the
suggestion*)
GEORGE: You mean that you'd meet Carrel and …
FENTON: … And tell him precisely what I know – then
             I should insist that he got in touch with me the
             moment he heard from Gallegos.
GEORGE: It's quite an idea, sir!
GRAYSON: I couldn't sanction a thing like that! You
             know that Bellamy.
(*The telephone rings. GRAYSON turns back to his desk and
lifts the receiver*)
GRAYSON: (*On phone*) Hello? … Yes, I'll hold on …

123

FENTON: Well, it was just an idea. (*He looks at his watch*) It's about time I made a move. Goodbye, sir.

GEORGE: (*To GRAYSON*) Good-bye, sir.

GRAYSON: Oh, good-bye.

(*FENTON and GEORGE leave*)

GRAYSON: (*On phone*) Hello? … Oh, hello, Mary! … No, very late … I'm sorry … Well, put it back in the oven – all right then, take it out of the oven … Darling, I'm sorry – it just can't be helped.

(*He notices a document on his desk; he starts to read it; hardly realises that he is on the phone*)

GRAYSON: All right, Mary … Yes, dear … Yes, of course, dear … Good-bye, dear.

(*He replaces the receiver and continues reading. GEORGE returns, crosses to the desk and picks up FENTON's gloves*)

GEORGE: He forgot his gloves.

GRAYSON: (*Looking up*) Oh.

(*GEORGE turns away from the desk and then hesitates*)

GEORGE: That was a good idea of his, wasn't it?

GRAYSON: About contacting Carrel? (*Nods*) Very.

GEORGE: It's a pity in a way that we …

GRAYSON: I couldn't sanction a thing like that.

GEORGE: Of course not.

GRAYSON: If the A.C. heard about it, he'd go up in smoke!

GEORGE: Yes, of course.

GRAYSON: I mean, a thing like that would have to be unofficial. Completely unofficial.

GEORGE: Oh, completely. (*A slight pause*) Well, I'll see you later, sir.

GRAYSON: Yes, all right, Bellamy.

(*They give each other an understanding look*)

CUT TO: FENTON's office.

SISTER ROGERS is sitting at the desk writing a letter; she finishes it and puts it in an envelope. The telephone rings and she lifts the receiver. There are several X-ray plates on the desk.

SISTER: (*On phone*) Hello? … Yes … Dr Craig? … No, I'm afraid he isn't … Can I take a message? … Yes – yes, of course … Oh, I see … Well, I'd better get Dr Craig to give you a ring … Western 3127? … Yes, all right. I'll tell him. Good-bye.

(*SISTER replaces the receiver. FENTON has entered whilst she was on the telephone*)

SISTER: That was a Mr Bingley – for Dr Craig.

FENTON: Oh, I see.

SISTER: It was something about a car.

FENTON: Oh. (*He looks down at the X-ray plates*)

SISTER: Is Dr Craig buying a new car?

FENTON: (*Looking up*) What do you mean, a new one? He hasn't got a car.

SISTER: Yes, he has. He took me out in it about a week ago.

FENTON: Oh, that's not his, it belongs to a friend of his.

SISTER: (*Laughing; nodding at the telephone*) That's not what Mr Bingley thinks.

FENTON: What do you mean?

SISTER: He was talking about taking it in part exchange.

FENTON: (*Puzzled*) Oh. (*Suddenly; closing the subject*) Perhaps I'm wrong.

(*CRAIG enters*)

CRAIG: Matron wants to see you, Sister.

SISTER: Thanks.

FENTON: There's been a call for you, Craig – from a Mr Bingley. (*He is watching Craig*)

CRAIG: Bingley?

FENTON: Yes, it was something to do with a car. What was the number, Sister?

SISTER: He'd like you to ring him. Western 3127.

CRAIG: (*Suddenly; amused*) Oh, Bingley! That silly old fool! He's as mad as a hatter!

SISTER: (*To CRAIG*) How's Mr Armitage?

CRAIG: (*Delighted*) He's worse this morning, Sister.

(*SISTER ROGERS laughs and leaves*)

CRAIG: You look very serious.

FENTON: What was all that about a car?

CRAIG: (*Smiling*) I don't know. Didn't you ask Mr Bingley?

FENTON: Sister took the call.

CRAIG: Well, didn't you ask Sister?

FENTON: (*Petulantly*) No, of course I didn't. It's no business of mine.

CRAIG: Well, what are you worried about?

FENTON: I'm not worried. I was just wondering how you could afford to buy a new car, that's all. (*Takes X-ray plates from the desk*) Craig, I want you to take a look at this plate. It came through from Gillespie this morning with a note from Professor Lewiston …

CRAIG: I've seen it. I saw it first thing this morning. It's a lot of nonsense. (*Smiling*) Fenton, I've got a pleasant surprise for you.

FENTON: Oh?

(*CRAIG takes FENTON's cheque out of his pocket*)

CRAIG: I shan't be needing the hundred pounds …

FENTON: Oh …

CRAIG: (*Tearing the cheque into little pieces*) So you can forget all about it.

FENTON: But what happened?

CRAIG: My father kicked in with a couple of hundred and I borrowed the rest from somebody else.

FENTON: Oh – then you're all right?

CRAIG: Yes. I'm solvent. I'm even on speaking terms with my bank manager.

FENTON: I hope you keep it that way.

CRAIG: I'll try. He's got a beautiful daughter.

FENTON: (*Amused*) Craig, I'm beginning to think you're a bit of a bounder.

CRAIG: I'm a terrible bounder, old boy – didn't you know. Why, in my student days I was known as the Sheik of Sauchiehall Street. I daren't set foot in Glasgow – there'd be a curfew straight away.

FENTON: (*Laughing*) Yes, well as long as you're not known as the Sheik of St Matthew's.

CRAIG: Don't be silly. Have you seen the nurses in this establishment? There's only Sister Rogers and that blonde piece up in Ward 3 that's worth looking at.

FENTON: That blonde piece, as you so graphically put it, is leaving.

CRAIG: Oh!

FENTON: She was quite incompetent.

CRAIG: That wasn't my experience.

(*FENTON gives CRAIG a look. There is a 'buzz' on the house telephone. FENTON knocks down the switch and lifts the receiver*)

FENTON: (*On phone*) Yes? … Who? … Mrs Foster would like a word with you, Craig.

(*FENTON hands the receiver to CRAIG*)

CRAIG: (*On phone*) Hello! … I'll be right up. (*He replaces the receiver and turns towards the door*) See you later. (*Hesitates*) Oh, by the way, Fenton – don't think I wasn't grateful. About the hundred quid, I mean.

FENTON: If I'd known your reputation you woudn't have got a bob.

(*CRAIG laughs and goes out. FENTON looks at his watch; hesitates a moment and then picks up the telephone*)

FENTON: (*On phone*) Get me the Ritz Hotel, please (*A pause*) Ritz Hotel? … I want to speak to Mr Ernest Carrel please (*A pause*) Hello? … Mr Carrel? … Good morning, my name is Fenton. I'm sorry to trouble you, but a mutual friend asked me to get in touch with you … No, I'm afraid I can't – not over the phone … Well, couldn't we meet somewhere and have a drink? … I told you – a mutual friend. (*Smiles*) His name was Carl Brunner …

CUT TO: *ERNEST CARREL is on the telephone in his suite in the Ritz Hotel. The telephone is on a stand; a closed suitcase is on a table with slats nearby. CARREL is dressed, except for the jacket of his suit.*

CARREL: (*On phone*) What name did you say? … (*quietly*) I see … All right – we'd better meet tonight sometime … Yes, I know it. It's just off Curzon Street, isn't it? … Yes, all right … nine o'clock …

(*CARREL slowly replaces the receiver*)

CUT TO: A bar-lounge in Mayfair.
HARRY, a waiter, greets FENTON as he enters.
HARRY: Good evening, sir.
FENTON: Good evening.

HARRY: What can I get you, sir?

FENTON: I think I'll wait. I'm expecting a friend.

(*He sits in one of the armchairs*)

HARRY: Very good, sir.

FENTON: (*Changing his mind*) No, on second thoughts, I'll have a whisky and soda.

HARRY: Double, sir?

FENTON: Er – yes.

HARRY: Thank you, sir.

(*HARRY goes. FENTON glances at his wristlet watch; takes out his cigarette case; lights a cigarette. HARRY returns with a tray containing a syphon and whisky*)

HARRY: (*About to press the syphon*) Say 'when', sir. (*Works syphon*)

FENTON: Whoa! That's fine – thank you.

(*HARRY puts the syphon and the drink down on the table*)

FENTON: You're not very busy tonight.

HARRY: Yes, things are very quiet. They have been all day, sir.

(*CRAIG enters: wears a lounge suit. Looks very pleased with life; he has already had several drinks*)

HARRY: Good evening, doctor.

CRAIG: Good evening, Harry.

HARRY: The usual, sir?

CRAIG: The usual – only make it a double.

(*CRAIG sits on a stool at the bar*)

FENTON: What precisely are you celebrating, Dr Craig?

(*CRAIG turns and notices FENTON. HARRY mixes CRAIG's drink*)

CRAIG: Why, Fenton! The old maestro himself! What are you doing here?

FENTON: What's more to the point – what are you doing here?

(*HARRY hands CRAIG his drink*)

CRAIG: I'm celebrating, Mr Fenton. Celebrating! Do you know what happens tomorrow morning?

FENTON: No?

CRAIG: Do you know what happens at precisely eleven o'clock tomorrow morning?

FENTON: No.

CRAIG: Mr Armitage leaves the hospital.

FENTON: What!

CRAIG: (*Grinning*) It's true.

FENTON: Is he better?

CRAIG: Well, he thinks he is. (*Suddenly*) Now don't you go and disillusion him!

(*FENTON laughs*)

CRAIG: What are you going to have?

FENTON: I've got one, thanks. Anyhow I'm expecting a friend.

CRAIG: That's all right. I'll push off the moment he arrives.

FENTON: It isn't a 'he', it's a 'she'.

CRAIG: Oh. Blonde or brunette?

FENTON: Blonde.

CRAIG: And very nice too. I'm particularly amen … amena … What the devil's the word?

FENTON: The word's amenable.

CRAIG: That's right. Well, I'm particularly amenable to blondes.

FENTON: You seem particularly amenable to a great many things, Craig – including whisky.

CRAIG: Did you ever meet a Scotsman that wasn't? I mean a real Scotsman – not one of those Music-hall turns you English laugh your silly heads at!

FENTON: Mr Mortimer Charles Duncan Craig, you're a little the worse for drink, if you ask me.

CRAIG: (*Lifting his glass*) I'm never the worse for drink, old boy. Do you know the best whisky I've ever tasted?

FENTON: No.

CRAIG: McRogers Highland Malt. Delicious.

FENTON: Was that the whisky Jackie Leroy sent you?

CRAIG: Why, yes! Yes, now you come to mention it I believe it was. (*Smacking his lips*) McRogers Highland Malt. Delicious.

FENTON: I suppose you've heard about Jackie Leroy?

CRAIG: Heard what?

FENTON: She was murdered.

CRAIG: (*Stunned*) Jackie!

FENTON: Yes.

CRAIG: You're joking! But why should anyone want to murder her?

FENTON: I don't know why – but they did.

CRAIG: But that's fantastic, why ...

FENTON: Craig, do you remember what you said about Jackie?

CRAIG: No?

FENTON: You said – she knows everything that goes on in this Town and what she doesn't know she soon finds out.

CRAIG: Did – I say that?

FENTON: You did.

CRAIG: Is that why she was murdered? Because ... she found out something?

FENTON: (*After a moment*) In my opinion – yes.

CRAIG: I see.

FENTON: (*Quietly*) I wonder if you do see, Craig?

CRAIG: What do you mean?

FENTON: How well did you know Jackie?

CRAIG: I told you – hardly at all. We simply met at a party.

FENTON: Then why did she give you the four bottles of Scotch?

CRAIG: I don't know why. It was just one of those things. She took rather a fancy to me. (*Wistfully*) She called me Scottie.

FENTON: Yes, I know she did.

CRAIG: Poor Jackie ... It hardly seems possible. When did it happen, Fenton – do you know?

FENTON: (*Nodding*) On Thursday. Sometime between five and half past six.

CRAIG: (*Nodding; thoughtfully*) That was the day I was with Dr Gillespie and Sister Rogers. We were together from four o'clock until half past eight.

FENTON: Why are you telling me that?

CRAIG: Don't you know why? Because you've got a brother-in-law at Scotland Yard. I'm making sure he doesn't get any silly ideas.

(*CRAIG finishes his drink and rises*)

CRAIG: Well, I'll be seeing you, Fenton.

(*CRAIG moves from the bar; then turns*)

CRAIG: I don't suppose those blondes of yours have got a girlfriend, by any chance?

FENTON: I doubt it, Craig – very much.

CRAIG: Bad show. Goodnight, Harry.

HARRY: Good night, doctor.

(*CRAIG goes. Another customer arrives and takes the stool on which CRAIG was sitting. HARRY serves him. CARREL enters and stands at the bar*)

HARRY: Good evening, sir.

CARREL: A brandy, please.

FENTON: Will you have it with me, Mr Carrel?

CARREL: Mr Fenton?

132

FENTON: Yes. Shall we sit down?

(*They move to a table*)

FENTON: (*Smiling*) I gather I'm not what you expected?

CARREL: Not exactly.

FENTON: What did you expect – someone like Mr Constance?

(*There is a look of surprise from CARREL when FENTON mentions Constance*)

CARREL: More or less. Blackmailers usually run to type.

FENTON: I'm the exception.

CARREL: In appearance, yes. But not when we get down to 'business'.

FENTON: It's only when we get down to 'business' that you'll realise just how exceptional I am.

(*HARRY arrives with CARREL's drink and he puts it down on the table*)

CARREL: Thank you.

(*FENTON pays HARRY*)

CARREL: Was Constance a friend of yours?

FENTON: An acquaintance.

CARREL: (*Sips his drink*) On the phone you mentioned the name of a mutual friend.

FENTON: (*Shaking his head*) We have no mutual friend. The name I mentioned was Carl Brunner. You used that name in Zurich in May '45.

CARREL: (*After a moment*) Did Constance tell you that?

FENTON: No.

CARREL: Who did?

FENTON: That's not important.

CARREL: (*Watching him*) What else do you know?

FENTON: Morton Smith, Lisbon, June '46.

CARREL: Go on …

FENTON: Morton Smith called himself a publicity expert. I'm told that the Portuguese authorities are still looking for him.

CARREL: (*Slowly*) Supposing I say I've never heard of Carl Brunner, that the name Morton Smith doesn't mean anything to me?

FENTON: Then I should ask you what you were doing here? You only came because I mentioned the name Carl Brunner.

(*CARREL sips his drink again; he looks at FENTON over the top of the glass*)

CARREL: (*Cynically*) If I give you what you want – how do I know you'll keep your mouth shut?

FENTON: How did you know that Constance would?

CARREL: (*Hesitating*) I didn't know – I had to take a chance on it. In any case, Constance didn't ask for money – not at first.

FENTON: (*Shaking his head*) Then he and I have something in common after all. I'm not asking for it either.

CARREL: (*Puzzled*) What do you mean?

FENTON: (*Leaning forward*) Constance blackmailed you into allowing the Broken Horseshow crowd to dope 'Siesta'.

CARREL: (*A pause*) Well?

FENTON: Well, it's my bet that Gallegos and his friends will contact you again – and when they do I want to know about it.

CARREL: But, assuming that you're right, why should I tell you about it?

FENTON: (*Smiling*) Because that's my price. I'm not demanding money from you; I'm simply asking you to co-operate.

CARREL: (*Puzzled*) Are you the police?

FENTON: No, I've told you who I am. My name is Fenton. I'm a surgeon at St Matthew's Hospital.

CARREL: A surgeon?

FENTON: Yes. (*Drinks his whisky*)

CARREL: (*Leaning forward*) Look, let's get this straight. What exactly is it you want me to do?

FENTON: Gallegos, or one of the gang, will get in touch with you. You agree to do what they want, and then ...

CARREL: Pass the information on to you?

FENTON: (*Nods*) It's as simple as that.

CARREL: (*Amazed*) And if I do that you'll forget all about Carl Brunner and Morton Smith?

FENTON: (*Nodding*) All about them. (*Smiling*) I never did have a very good memory for names.

CARREL: You know, I'm damned if I know whether to take you seriously or not.

FENTON: You'd be well advised to, Mr Carrel. (*Smiling*) If you don't you know the alternative.

(*CARREL slowly strokes his chin*)

CARREL: Yes – I see your point.

CUT TO: *CRAIG is sitting on a corner of the desk, alone, in FENTON's office, on the telephone.*

CRAIG: (*On phone*) ... You're very obstinate this morning, Maureen ... Well, why not Tuesday? ... All right, let's make it Friday ... O.K. if you can't manage Friday, let's make it Saturday then ... My, you are booked up ... (*Laughing*) You know your trouble, Maureen – you've been eating too many apples ... No, apples ... That's right ... (*Smiles*) Well, I'm feeling corny ... (*Laughing*) You don't know what you're missing – I've got a new car ... Oh, about

135

three days ago … No, part exchange … Yes, one
of the new ones …

(*SISTER ROGERS enters. She is carrying a letter*)

CRAIG: (*Smiling at SISTER; still on the phone*) Yes, well
give me a ring one day next week … That's fine!
(*He replaces the receiver*)

SISTER: Have you seen Mr Fenton?

CRAIG: He's in the examining room.

(*SISTER turns towards the door but CRAIG stops her*)

CRAIG: What a moment! Don't rush away – I'm not
contagious.

SISTER: I've got work to do.

CRAIG: We've all got work to do, but nobody's going to
die if you relax for a moment. (*Grinning*) Have
you got a date on Tuesday?

SISTER: No.

CRAIG: How would you like to come out with me? I've
got a new car.

SISTER: No, thank you. I was in your old car once,
remember.

CRAIG: Yes, but this is much better, it's much more
roomy.

SISTER: It's not roomy enough for me, Dr Craig!

(*CRAIG laughs. SISTER ROGERS moves in front of glass
door. CRAIG follows her*)

CRAIG: Wait a minute, Sister. If you don't want to go out
in my car, why don't you come out with me and
have a bite to eat?

SISTER: Dr Craig, when will it penetrate that large swollen
head of yours that I'm not your type?

CRAIG: But you <u>are</u> my type, Sister. That's what I keep
telling you. I don't go for these fluffy little things.

SISTER: You went for that fluffy little night nurse!

CRAIG: That's a long time ago. Frankly, Sister, don't I arouse any interest in you? Not even the maternal instinct?

SISTER: Dr Craig, in another ten years, you'll be what's commonly called a roué.

(*She leaves through the glass door*)

CRAIG: (*Laughing*) Well, thanks for the ten years, anyway.

(*FENTON enters; his manner is brisk; he carries a stethoscope*)

FENTON: (*To CRAIG*) I thought you were on rounds?

CRAIG: Rounds? Oh yes of course – Rounds!

(*CRAIG leaves as SISTER ROGERS returns*)

FENTON: (*To SISTER*) Did you want me, Sister?

SISTER: Yes, I've been looking for you, Mr Fenton. The Porter asked me to give you this letter.

FENTON: Thank you.

(*FENTON takes the letter. SISTER ROGERS goes. FENTON opens the envelope and reads the letter. His expression gradually denotes surprise and anxiety. He quickly picks up the telephone receiver*)

FENTON: (*On phone*) Get me Scotland Yard, please – quickly! Ask for Inspector Bellamy … It's urgent!

CUT TO: CARREL's Suite at the Ritz Hotel.

CARREL enters carrying a sheet, pillow, etc. He looks dejected, unshaven and is smoking a cigarette. CARREL goes to the fireplace and then crosses to a table and takes a drink. He goes to the door and locks it and puts the sheet at the bottom of the door. He crosses to the window and draws the curtains. He takes the pillow and drops it in front of the fire, then crosses to the drinks table and finishes his drink and stubs out the cigarette. He bends down and turns on the gas and lowers himself slowly onto the pillow.

CUT TO: FENTON's Office.

FENTON is still on the telephone.

FENTON: (*On phone*) George? This is Mark … Listen! I've had a letter from Carrel … I can't tell you what it says   over the phone but we've got to see him, George … Yes, it's urgent … Yes, I can … All right, I'll see you at the hotel.

(*FENTON replaces the receiver and commences to take off his white jacket*)

CUT TO: CARREL's Suite at the Ritz Hotel.

CARREL is still on the floor, motionless, by the gas fire. The gas is still pouring into the room. Voices can be heard in the corridor outside; GEORGE starts to knock on the door.

FENTON: (*Voice from outside the room*) You can smell the gas, George!

GEORGE: (*Voice from outside the room*) My God, yes! (*Banging on the door*) Open the door! Open the door, Carrel!

CUT TO: *FENTON, GEORGE and the RECEPTIONIST at the door of CARREL's SUITE. GEORGE is banging on the door.*

FENTON: (*To RECEPTIONIST*) Haven't you got a pass key?

RECEPTIONIST: (*Nervous; confused*) A pass k-key?

(*GEORGE turns on the RECEPTIONIST; tense; a shade angry*)

GEORGE: Yes, a pass key. Look, we've got to get in this ruddy room! Do you want us to break the door down!

RECEPTIONIST: You'd better try these, sir!

(*The RECEPTIONIST takes a bunch of keys out of his pocket. GEORGE snatches them*)

CUT TO: Inside CARREL's SUITE at the RITZ Hotel.
The door is suddenly thrown opens and FENTON and GEORGE followed by the RECEPTIONIST burst into the room. GEORGE crosses to the window and throws it open. FENTON, handkerchief to mouth, rushes across to the fire and turns off the gas. The RECEPTIONIST goes into the bedroom and opens the windows.

CUT TO: *FELIX GALLEGOS is in a telephone box, about to insert coins in the press-button box. He inserts coins then dials. A pause. GALLEGOS presses button "A"*

GALLEGOS: Ritz Hotel? I want to speak to Mr Ernest Carrel, please.

CUT TO: CARREL's SUITE at the RITZ Hotel. As before.
FENTON comes out of the bedroom; he looks worried. GEORGE turns towards him. FENTON takes the letter out of his pocket.

FENTON: If we'd been ten minutes earlier. We might have saved him, George. (*Holds out the letter*) Here's the letter he sent me; you'd better take it.

GEORGE: What does it say?

(*FENTON looks down at the letter; hesitates*)

FENTON: (*Reading*) 'Dear Fenton … I've thought quite a lot about what you said last night, but I realise now that there's only one way out, and I've got to take it. You see, I murdered Charles Constance. I thought that once he was out of the way things would be different, but somehow it just didn't pan out that way. It's strange to think that less than eight weeks ago I felt so safe. I haven't yet heard from the Broken Horseshoe but I suspect that you're

139

right and that they will contact me. This time
they'll be too late …… Ernest Carrel' …

(*FENTON looks up from the letter*)

FENTON: So he murdered Constance.

GEORGE: Yes. We've had our eye on Carrel for some
time now. Apparently the day that …

(*The telephone starts to ring. GEORGE looks at FENTON:
lifts the receiver*)

GEORGE: (*On phone*) Yes? … Well, put him on … (*To
FENTON*) It's a call for Carrel.

(*FENTON stands close to GEORGE so that he can hear what
is said over the telephone*)

GEORGE: (*On phone*) Hello? … Yes? … Yes – this is
Ernest Carrel speaking.

CUT TO: *FELIX GALLEGOS is in the telephone box; he
holds an unlighted cigarette in his left hand as he speaks.*

GALLEGOS: Mr Carrel? … My name is Gallegos. I think
perhaps you've heard of me. (*Smiling*) Yes …
Yes … We'd like to see you. We have a
proposition to make … Well, there's no
particular hurry. Let's say Thursday morning
– yes, Thursday … No, no, not at your hotel,
Mr Carrel. We want you to come to St
Matthew's Hospital – yes, in Kensington …
That's right, St Matthew's on Thursday
morning. (*Smiles*) Ask for Mr Mark   Fenton.

(*GALLEGOS replaces the receiver; puts the unlighted
cigarette in his mouth. The door of the phone box opens
slightly and a man's hand stretches across from the right,
flicks a cigarette lighter and offers GALLEGOS a light. We do
not see the man*)

END OF PART FIVE

Part Six:

OPERATION HORSESHOE

OPEN TO: *FELIX GALLEGOS is in the telephone box. He holds an unlighted cigarette in his left hand as he speaks.*

GALLEGOS: No, no, not at your hotel, Mr Carrel. We want you to come to St Matthew's Hospital – yes, in Kensington … That's right, St Matthew's on Thursday morning. (*Smiles*) Ask for Mr Mark Fenton.

(*GALLEGOS replaces the receiver; puts the unlighted cigarette in his mouth. The door of the phone box opens slightly and a man's hand stretches across from the right, flicks a cigarette lighter and offers GALLEGOS a light. We do not see the man*)

GALLEGOS: What are you doing here? I told you I'd do it, didn't I? You don't leave anything to chance, do you, my friend?

CUT TO: ERNEST CARREL's Suite.

GEORGE replaces the telephone receiver. FENTON is standing by his side.

GEORGE: Did you hear that?

FENTON: (*Puzzled*) Yes – Why should they want Carrel to ask for me? In any case, I'm not at the hospital on Thursday. I'm away all day seeing patients.

(*GEORGE is thoughtful. He crosses to the chair near the drinks table*)

GEORGE: Gallegos is a pretty smooth character.

FENTON: What do you think happened when Carrel murdered Constance?

GEORGE: You can see what happened, Mark. Constance arranged to meet Carrel at the flat – obviously meaning to blackmail him again, only this time for money. But Carrel murdered him and then, to divert suspicion from himself,

143

	planted the Broken Horseshoe sign on the mirror.
FENTON:	But the sign wasn't there when I got back to the flat.
GEORGE:	No, because Della Freeman wiped it off.
FENTON:	But she didn't get as far as the flat, I met her in the hall.
GEORGE:	(*Shaking his head*) She had already been in the flat when you saw her.
FENTON:	How do you know?
GEORGE:	One of the porters saw her – and though he didn't realise who she was he gave us an accurate description.
FENTON:	Then she must have seen the body …
GEORGE:	Yes, it all ties up. Carrel murders Constance, puts the sign on the mirror and departs. Later Della arrives, realises what's happened, and, since she's new in the Broken Horseshoe gang, immediately removes the horseshoe from the mirror.
FENTON:	Yes, that would account for the slip she made when she was talking to me. She said Constance had been strangled, when I only said he'd been murdered.

(*GEORGE nods; picks up the telephone receiver*)

| GEORGE: | Yes. (*On phone*) Will you get me Whitehall 1212, please? Ask for Superintendent Grayson. (*Replaces receiver*) |
| FENTON: | I'm beginning to understand. (*Thoughtfully*) Della knew that Constance had something on Carrel but she wasn't sure what it was. (*GEORGE nods*) Without Constance realising it, she double-crossed him and played in with the Broken Horseshoe. |

144

GEORGE: Exactly.

FENTON: But how did my cigarette lighter get by the body?

GEORGE: Yes, that's a point that still puzzles me.

FENTON: Have you a warrant out for Gallegos?

GEORGE: (*Nodding*) And the girl – but they seem to have picked a pretty good hide-out.

FENTON: Of course it beats me how you people ever find anybody in a city this size.

GEORGE: We shall pick the girl up, I'm pretty sure about that – but I'm not sure about Gallegos.

(*The telephone rings. GEORGE lifts the receiver*)

GEORGE: (*On phone*) Hello? … Oh, good evening, sir. Bellamy here … No – he wasn't. He left a message for us … I was wondering if you'd heard anything from the airports, sir … No … No, I don't think so … Oh, good! … Yes, I'll be right back … (*Replaces the receiver. To FENTON*) Sergeant West has picked up Della Freeman – she was in a café on the Edgware Road.

CUT TO: SUPERINTENDENT GRAYSON's Office at Scotland Yard.

DELLA FREEMAN is sitting in the armchair facing the desk. GRAYSON is standing by the desk.

GRAYSON: You found a good hideout, young lady. We've been searching for you for some time.

DELLA: I've been staying with my sister at Drayton Court.

GRAYSON: (*Shaking his head*) You haven't got a sister. The flat at Drayton Court was taken by you two months ago in the name of Kelsey. You lived there with Constance until you decided

145

to double-cross him and throw in your lot with Gallegos. (*Turning; his back to the desk*) You haven't been near that flat since the day Constance was murdered.

DELLA: You seem to be well informed.

(*GRAYSON smiles; takes papers from the desk*)

GRAYSON: I make a point of being well informed. (*Holding out papers*) You must find London pretty dull at this time of the year.

DELLA: What do you mean?

GRAYSON: Isn't the South of France your stamping ground? (*Looks at papers*) You appear to have spent a great deal of time there. May, June, July, August, September, '49. August, September, '50. February, March, July, August, '51. You must know that coast pretty well, Miss Mason.

DELLA: My name is Della Freeman.

GRAYSON: Not according to my information. You certainly didn't tell that young fellow in Juan-les-Pins that your name was Freeman. You know the one I'm talking about – the one that committed suicide.

DELLA: He'd been gambling – he lost a lot of money at the Casino. Was it my fault if he jumped from the hotel window?

GRAYSON: It depends which way you look at it. (*Puts papers down on the desk*) However, I didn't bring you here to discuss the South of France.

DELLA: Then why did you bring me here?

GRAYSON: (*After a moment*) What do you know about the murder of Jackie Leroy?

DELLA: (*Obviously surprised*) What are you talking about?

146

GRAYSON: You arranged to see Dr Fenton at a house in Ellsworth Crescent; when Fenton arrived there, he found the body of Jackie Leroy.

DELLA: I don't know anyone called Leroy.

GRAYSON: I think you do, Miss Mason. Now look – (*Indicates the papers on his desk*) – I've got your history. I know your whole story. I know what happened when you left that school in Switzerland, I know about the Deauville incident, about the boy at Juan-les-Pins. It's not a very pleasant story, let's face it – but so far, if we exclude Constance and the Jackie Leroy incident, it doesn't include murder.

DELLA: I've told you, I've never heard of Miss Leroy.

GRAYSON: Then what makes you think Jackie Leroy is a woman? Now look, so far as you're concerned we're interested in two things – and two things only. Who murdered Jackie Leroy, and the whereabouts of Felix Gallegos.

DELLA: (*A shade angry*) I don't know what you're talking about. I tell you I've never heard of anyone called Jackie Leroy. And who's this Felix Gallegos?

GRAYSON: All right, if that's the way you want it!

(*GEORGE enters*)

GEORGE: (*To GRAYSON*) Sorry I'm late, Sir. It took longer than I expected.

GRAYSON: (*Nodding to DELLA*) She refuses to co-operate. She's never heard of Jackie Leroy.

GEORGE: (*Pleasantly*) Really? Then that confirms my suspicions. Gallegos is lying.

DELLA: What do you mean?

GEORGE: We've just picked up Felix Gallegos. He said that you murdered Jackie Leroy.

147

DELLA:	(*Rising; angry*) That's a lie! You're bluffing!
GEORGE:	(*Smiling*) That's exactly what I said to Gallegos.
DELLA:	What do you mean?
GEORGE:	I said I didn't believe you'd murdered Jackie Leroy. I still don't believe it. You may have murdered Constance, but so far as Jackie was concerned ...
DELLA:	(*Tensely*) I didn't murder Constance!
GEORGE:	(*Quickly*) Then who did?
DELLA:	(*After a moment*) Ernest Carrel. Constance was blackmailing him. I arrived at the flat just after Mr Fenton had left, as a matter of fact I saw him running to the phone box. As soon as I saw Constance, I guessed what had happened and made a quick search for the railway ticket – although at that time I was actually looking for a document of some sort.
GEORGE:	And then?
DELLA:	(*Hesitating; looking at GEORGE*) Did Gallegos really say that I'd murdered Jackie Leroy?
GEORGE:	(*Nodding*) Go on, Miss Freeman.
DELLA:	Well, I saw the sign on the mirror and realised that Carrel had put it there to throw suspicion on to the Broken Horseshoe, so as I'd already decided to play in with Gallegos I rubbed out the sign.
GEORGE:	But why did you go back to the flat?
DELLA:	Because on my way home it suddenly dawned on me that Fenton knew about Constance and was phoning for the police. I was curious. I wondered what Fenton was doing at Drayton Court and if by any chance Constance had

148

given him the information I'd been searching for. It was just the sort of thing Constance would do. I made up my mind to find out. I jumped into a taxi and returned to the block of flats. I was lucky, the timing was perfect. I got out of the taxi and into the hall just as Fenton came back from the telephone box.

GEORGE: I see.

GRAYSON: Who tried to murder Constance in the first place?

DELLA: You mean the car accident? That was Carrel – but I tried to convince Constance it was the Broken Horseshoe gang. You see, soon after the accident Gallegos came to see me. He asked me to deliver the card with the Broken Horseshoe on it. He thought it might frighten Constance into handing over his information about Ernest Carrel.

GRAYSON: But Constance wasn't easily frightened.

GEORGE: No. If I could forget he was a blackmailer I should take rather a favourable view of him. I think he got rather a raw deal.

GRAYSON: (*To GEORGE*) Where did you pick up Gallegos?

GEORGE: About an hour ago.

GRAYSON: No, I said where?

GEORGE: Oh, we got a hot tip late this afternoon and we went along to the … er …

(*GEORGE puts his hand on his brow; clicks his fingers*)

GEORGE: To the … er … (*Turns to Della; quite casually*) What the devil was the name of that place?

DELLA: Hotel Stewart.

GEORGE: (*Nodding; business like*) Thank you, Miss
                Freeman. (*To GRAYSON*) She's right about
                Carrel – he did murder Constance. But I'm
                afraid we haven't picked up Gallegos.
DELLA: What!
GEORGE: Don't worry, Miss Freeman – we soon will.
(*GEORGE picks up the telephone on the desk and dials one
letter on the dial*)
GEORGE: (*On phone*) Inspector Bellamy speaking – I
                want a Squad car … Yes, straight away! (*He
                smiles at GRAYSON*)

CUT TO: Interior corner of a Barber's shop at the Hotel
Stewart.
*GALLEGOS is lying full length in the barber's chair; hot
towels completely cover his features. The BARBER is
standing near the wash-basin drying his hands on a towel.
There are several pegs on a nearby wall, from one of which
hangs GALLEGOS's jacket. GEORGE and a PLAIN-
CLOTHES SERGEANT are sitting to the right of the barber's
chair, apparently awaiting their turn. GEORGE is reading a
newspaper, quite unconcerned. A door is heard opening. The
BARBER looks up.*
BARBER: I'm sorry, sir – we're closed.
(*The door closes*)
BARBER: (*To GEORGE*) I won't keep you long now,
            sir.
GEORGE: That's all right. I'm in no hurry.
(*The BARBER slowly removes the towels from GALLEGOS's
face; then straightens the chair. GALLEGOS sits up;   looks
straight into the camera – using it as a mirror. Pats his face,
pinches his cheeks; appears satisfied. He rises, fastens his
collar; studies himself in the invisible mirror as he knots his
tie. GEORGE   and   the   SERGEANT   sit   watching   him.*

Eventually GALLEGOS turns and takes his jacket from the peg. He is about to put it on when he stops and feels the right-hand side pocket – and realises his revolver is missing. For a brief moment he looks very startled. GEORGE rises; takes the revolver out of his pocket)

GEORGE: Is this what you're looking for, Mr Gallegos?

GALLEGOS: What the devil is this? Who are you?

GEORGE: (*Showing GALLEGOS a card which he holds in his left hand*) Inspector Bellamy, Scotland Yard.

CUT TO: FENTON's Office.

FENTON enters, followed by SISTER ROGERS. FENTON seems a little unsteady on his feet; giving the impression of being dizzy. He stands in the doorway for a moment, his hands covering his eyes.

SISTER: Are you all right, Mr Fenton?

FENTON: Yes, I think so.

SISTER: What happened?

FENTON: I don't know exactly. I was walking down the corridor and I suddenly felt dizzy. It's a good job I wasn't in the theatre. (*Smiles*) I'll be all right, Sister. I've been over-doing things I expect.

SISTER: What you need is a jolly good holiday.

FENTON: That's what we all need.

SISTER: Yes, but you do need a holiday, Mr Fenton, you've been working too hard.

FENTON: Yes, well, I'm taking my leave early this year – I'm off in a fortnight.

SISTER: Good. And take my advice, don't hang about the   hospital like you did last year.

FENTON: The way I'm feeling at the moment I shall probably jump in a plane and go straight to the Wilds of Borneo.

SISTER: Yes, and the first thing you'll do when you get there is pop to the local hospital!

FENTON: I'm glad you said hospital, Sister!

(*SISTER ROGERS laughs. CRAIG enters; he looks a shade perturbed*)

CRAIG: (*To FENTON*) What's all this I hear about you passing out?

FENTON: It's nothing, Craig.

CRAIG: But what happened?

FENTON: (*Sitting at his desk*) I had a dizzy spell, that's all. I didn't pass out.

CRAIG: Are you feeling all right now?

FENTON: Yes, I'm fine.

(*CRAIG glances across at the SISTER*)

SISTER: I shall be in Surgery if you want me, Mr Fenton.

FENTON: (*Nodding*) Thank you, Sister.

(*SISTER ROGERS looks at CRAIG and then goes out. FENTON puts his hand over his eyes again. CRAIG watches him for a moment*)

CRAIG: Are you sure you're feeling all right?

FENTON: (*Lowering his hand*) Yes – it's nothing.

CRAIG: I'm not sure about that. Have you had this sort of thing before?

FENTON: Not for some time.

CRAIG: But you have had it before?

FENTON: Yes.

CRAIG: When – exactly?

FENTON: Oh, two or three months ago. Forget it, Craig. It was probably something I didn't eat.

CRAIG: (*Nodding his head*) I know. It's the old story. You surgeons are all alike. You go on and on and on …

152

But you've got to remember, Fenton, that the human body is a delicate instrument and like most delicate instruments it's got to be taken care of.

FENTON: Well, well, you have got the bedside manner, Craig!

CRAIG: (*Smiling*) When was the last time you saw your doctor?

FENTON: I haven't got a doctor. (*Confidentially; 'pulling his leg'*) Strictly between ourselves, I don't believe in them.

CRAIG: Famous last words! Well, it's about time you started to believe in them.

FENTON: O.K., doc! I know you're looking for business. (*Nodding*) You can run the rule over me.

CRAIG: Seriously, I think it might be a good idea.

FENTON: Perhaps you're right. (*Hand over eyes for a moment*) When would you like to see me?

CRAIG: Are you on tonight?

FENTON: Yes, I shall be here until – oh, about eleven.

CRAIG: Then supposing I drop in about eleven o'clock?

FENTON: That'll do nicely.

CRAIG: (*Rises*) Fine! Well, I suppose I'd better do my rounds. See you tonight!

(*CRAIG goes out. FENTON watches him go*)

CUT TO: Corner of a hospital room.

SISTER ROGERS is sitting in an armchair reading a book. There is a telephone by her side, on a small table. She looks up, and rises, as Dr CRAIG comes into view. CRAIG carries his stethoscope and portable blood pressure apparatus.

SISTER: You're working late tonight, doctor.

CRAIG: Yes – I'm just going to take a look at Fenton.

SISTER: Oh – is there anything really wrong, do you think?

153

CRAIG: I don't know, but he didn't look too good this
            morning?
SISTER: No, he didn't.
CRAIG: If the Matron or Dr Turner should want to see me
            tell them I'm with Fenton.
SISTER: Don't worry, I'll see you're not disturbed.
CRAIG: (*Nods*) Thanks, Sister
(*CRAIG goes. SISTER sits down and is about to read her
book again when the telephone rings*)
SISTER: (*On phone*) Hello? ... Yes, speaking ... No, I'm
            sorry he's with Mr Fenton and can't be disturbed
            ... All right, I'll tell Dr Turner ... Yes, all right ...
            No, Matron's off duty ... Yes, very well.
            (*Replaces receiver; rises, shakes her head. She
            looks irritated*) Really, some people ...

CUT TO: FENTON's Office.
*CRAIG is lounging in the armchair looking up at FENTON
who is in the process of rolling down his shirt sleeves. During
the following scenes, FENTON puts on his white jacket which
is hanging over the back of his chair. There is now a small
bowl of flowers on the desk, facing the armchair.*
FENTON: Well, I take it I'm not going to die.
CRAIG: Not yet. (*Puzzled*) As a matter of fact, I can't find
            a thing the matter with you.
FEMTON: I told you it was nothing.
CRAIG: Well, it must be something, Fenton. You don't
            get dizzy spells like that without a reason.
FENTON: (*Sitting in his chair behind the desk*) I was over
            tired, I expect. Anyway, thanks for looking me
            over, Craig.
CRAIG: I should take it steady for the next two or three
            days.
FENTON: Easier said than done.

CRAIG: Yes, I know.

FENTON: Don't go, Craig – there's no hurry. Let Turner do some work for a change.

CRAIG: (*Relaxing*) By George, yes! He gets away with murder, that young fellow!

(*FENTON laughs*)

FENTON: Talking of murder, did you read about that fellow Constance?

CRAIG: Yes, I did! What an extraordinary thing. Have the police any idea who did it?

FENTON: Yes – a man called Carrel.

CRAIG: Not Ernest Carrel?

FENTON: Yes. Do you know him?

CRAIG: I met him at a party once – oh, a year or so ago. Seemed rather a decent type, I thought. Rolling in money.

FENTON: Yes.

CRAIG: But why should Carrel want to murder a man like Charles Constance?

FENTON: I don't know the whole story, but apparently Constance was blackmailing him. He blackmailed him into doping his horse 'Siesta'.

CRAIG: Did he, by jove? I won a fiver on that filly.

FENTON: Yes, my brother-in-law won six pounds ten.

(*CRAIG laughs*)

CRAIG: Was Constance anything to do with this gang the papers are taking about – the Broken Horseshoe?

FENTON: No, I understand he worked separately, although a man called Gallegos, one of the Broken Horseshoe crowd, tried to get Constance to hand him information about Carrel.

CRAIG: (*Laughing*) He obviously wanted to have a go at Carrel himself.

FENTON: Yes.

CRAIG: They sound a pretty lively bunch of characters.

FENTON: Oh, they're lively all right. But in my opinion there's somebody else behind this crowd.

CRAIG: What do you mean? (*Amused*) The Master Mind?

FENTON: I think Gallegos was the master mind as you call it, he certainly controlled things; but there's somebody else behind the Broken Horseshoe, there must be.

CRAIG: What do you mean?

FENTON: They used Penomycitin on 'Siesta'. You know as well as I do that isn't an easy drug to get hold of.

CRAIG: It certainly isn't. Are you sure they used Penomycitin?

FENTON: (*Watching him*) Yes – I've seen the report.

CRAIG: Well, I suppose there's a black market in drugs the same as anything else.

FENTON: Yes, but George doesn't think they get the stuff from the black market.

CRAIG: George?

FENTON: My brother-in-law, Inspector Bellamy.

CRAIG: Oh. Well, where does he think they get it from?

FENTON: (*Quietly*) One of the hospitals.

(*He takes out his cigarette case; offers CRAIG a cigarette*)

CRAIG: (*Taking a cigarette*) One of the hospitals! I say – that's a pretty serious accusation.

FENTON: It's a pretty serious business.

CRAIG: (*Thoughtfully*) Penomycitin. (*Gives a low whistle*) No wonder 'Siesta' won. I'd win the Grand National if they pumped that stuff into me.

(*FENTON takes out his lighter*)

FENTON: So you see what I mean?

CRAIG: Yes. I do indeed. You think the person behind Gallegos worked in a hospital. Probably a Sister, or a Matron, or …

156

FENTON: … one of the doctors.

CRAIG: And they supplied the stuff to Gallegos?

FENTON: (*Leaning forward; offering CRAIG a light*) Exactly.

CRAIG: (*Amused*) You know that's quite a theory, Fenton. You'd make a dashed good detective.

(*He accepts a light; notices the lighter*)

CRAIG: Oh, I see you've got your lighter back?

FENTON: Yes – (*Watching CRAIG*) – my brother-in-law found it.

CRAIG: It must be useful having a brother-in-law at Scotland Yard.

FENTON: It has advantages.

(*A moment*)

FENTON: I told you about Jackie Leroy's accident?

CRAIG: Yes.

FENTON: Well, apparently Jackie was mixed up in this business. As a matter of fact, I'm surprised you didn't know, Craig. I thought she was a friend of yours.

CRAIG: No, I told you, she wasn't a friend of mine.

FENTON: Oh, I thought she was. I remember you advised me to go and see her if I was in trouble at any time.

CRAIG: Did I?

FENTON: You did. As a matter of fact, I went. (*Smiling; significantly*) Mr Gallegos was there – waiting for me.

(*A pause*)

FENTON: Shortly after that interview with Gallegos you tried to borrow three hundred pounds.

CRAIG: (*Sits up*) What – do you mean, Fenton?

FENTON: You didn't need three hundred pounds, Craig.

CRAIG: Then why did I ask you for it?

157

FENTON: I told Gallegos I badly needed fifteen hundred and was prepared to sell the ticket for that sum.

CRAIG: Well?

FENTON: You were testing me. Unlike Gallegos you were not sure whether I needed the fifteen hundred or not. You thought I might have put one over on Mr Gallegos and was in fact playing in with Scotland Yard.

(*CRAIG rises*)

CRAIG: (*Looking down at FENTON*) Are you playing in with Scotland Yard, Fenton?

(*A pause*)

FENTON: (*Quietly*) Do you know when I suspected you – for the first time?

CRAIG: No?

FENTON: When I heard about the cigarette lighter; I knew you were the only person who could have taken it. You did take it, didn't you, Craig?

(*CRAIG sits on the desk; looking down at FENTON; a shade defiant*)

CRAIG: Yes, I did. I intended to murder Constance but when I got to the flat Carrel had already been there. I searched the flat and then placed the lighter by the side of the body. (*Grinning*) I was on my way out when Della Freeman arrived. We had quite an interesting little chat. I have a shrewd suspicion I'll be hearing from that young lady in the near future. However, I'll take care of that situation when it arises.

FENTON: It was you who telephoned me that night at Pinelio's, wasn't it?

CRAIG: Of course. I wanted to get you away from the table. I would have thought that was obvious.

(*CRAIG grins, in a strange kind of way, he looks rather pleased with himself*)

FENTON: Why did you make Gallegos tell Carrel to turn up at the hospital and ask for me?

CRAIG: I meant to blackmail Carrel. I knew you were off duty on Thursday and I told the receptionist to send your visitors to me.

(*He takes a revolver out of his pocket; it is fitted with a silencer*)

CRAIG: Don't underrate me, Fenton. Gallegos is a pretty shrewd customer but the Broken Horseshoe was my idea. I take full responsibility.

FENTON: (*Quietly; watching the revolver*) How much did you really make on 'Siesta'?

CRAIG: 'Siesta'? Nine thousand … But 'Faraway' was the best proposition – that was a beauty. Twelve and a half …

(*He looks thoughtful; suddenly angry*)

CRAIG: But it's all over now. Thanks to you.

FENTON: (*Softly*) Now don't be a fool, Craig! Put that revolver away!

(*CRAIG leans forward; holding the revolver out towards FENTON*)

CRAIG: Do you know what this is? It's a silencer … you'll hardly hear anything, Fenton. (*Grinning*) Just a dull, unpleasant little plop …

FENTON: Craig, are you crazy?

CRAIG: (*Softly; tensely*) Listen, I'll tell you what I'm going to do. After I've shot you, I'm going to take the silencer off and then put the revolver by the side of your body. Then I'm going outside and I'm going to have a nice little chat to Sister Rogers. I'm going to tell her you're in a very bad way, and musn't be disturbed – nerves all shot to pieces.

(*He grins*) Then I'm going upstairs, Fenton, to the little room just above this and I'm going to take another revolver – one without a silencer – and I'm going to fire it. Then I shall rush downstairs. Very excited … terribly distressed. (*Grinning*) But I shall let Sister Rogers discover the body …

FENTON: (*Staring at him*) My God, Craig! You really are crazy!

CRAIG: You shouldn't have interfered, Fenton. If you'd posted that letter and kept your nose out of this business you wouldn't have found yourself … in … this … particular …

(*CRAIG stops speaking; he is looking down at the bowl of flowers. FENTON rises*)

CRAIG: (*Pointing to the bowl of flowers*) What's this?

FENTON: It's a microphone, Craig. My brother-in-law's upstairs with Superintendent Grayson …

(*As he speaks, FENTON calmly leans forward and quietly takes the revolver out of CRAIG's hand*)

FENTON: There are two plain clothes men in the corridor …

(*CRAIG looks stunned*)

FENTON: (*Clicking the revolver*) We emptied this this morning, Craig – and the second one which we found in your locker.

(*The door opens. GEORGE enters, followed by SUPERINTENDENT GRAYSON. CRAIG turns towards the door. As soon as he sees GEORGE, he takes a capsule out of his pocket and puts it in his mouth. He bites on the capsule*)

GEORGE: (*To CRAIG*) Dr Craig? I'm Inspector Bellamy – this is Superintendent Grayson. We have a warrant for your arrest – and I must warn you that from now on anything you say will be taken …

(*CRAIG turns from the desk and sinks down on to the arm of the armchair*)

FENTON: Good Lord, he's taken something!

(*GEORGE and GRAYSON rush towards CRAIG*)

FENTON: Craig, what is it? What have you taken? What was in the capsule? (*Shakes CRAIG by the shoulder*) Craig!!!

(*CRAIG suddenly turns towards FENTON, then his head falls backwards. FENTON looks up at GEORGE and shakes his head*)

CUT TO: General view of London Airport.

CUT TO: A corner of the Departure Lounge at London Airport. There is a gay travel poster on a plain wall. *GEORGE is saying au-revoir to FENTON. A large   suitcase is on the floor complete with labels. GEORGE is wearing his trench coat. FENTON carries a brief case and several magazines. During this scene various BEA announcements can be heard over the loudspeakers.*

FENTON: It's very decent of you to see me off, George. I didn't expect this honour.

GEORGE: We've got to keep our eye on you, old boy – you're a pretty important witness. By the way, you'll be back by the end of next month, won't you?

FENTON: Good heavens, yes!

GEORGE: (*Smiling*) I've got some news for you, Mark. We picked up Carrel.

FENTON: When?

GEORGE: Yesterday afternoon. There was a race meeting at a small place called Cheslewood. Carrel just couldn't keep away from it.

FENTON: That was a pretty good hunch, George.

GEORGE: (*Holding out his hand*) I regret to say it was the Superintendent's. (*They shake hands*) Good-bye. Have a good time and take care of yourself.

FENTON: Good-bye. Keep your nose to the grindstone!

CUT TO: An aircraft's propellers revolving; crew near aircraft.

CUT TO: Interior of Aircraft cabin.

CONNIE HALIDAY is sitting in a window seat; she is a very attractive, sophisticated woman in her early thirties. There is a table facing her and a vacant seat. There is an ashtray on the table and magazines etc. FENTON arrives and puts his hat and brief case in the overhead rack; he looks down and notices CONNIE.

FENTON: (*Surprised*) Hello, Mrs Haliday!

CONNIE: (*Pleasantly surprised*) Why, hello, Mr Fenton!

FENTON: This is a surprise!

(*He takes the vacant seat*)

CONNIE: Do you know, I thought I saw you in the lounge! But I said to myself that can't be Mr Fenton. He's at the hospital working himself to death!

FENTON: Not this morning. I'm on vacation. I'm going to Nice for three weeks.

CONNIE: But how exciting!

FENTON: Are you going to Nice?

CONNIE: No, I'm going much further. Tunis.

FENTON: Oh.

CONNIE: My husband's in Tunis with the Sanderson Commission.

FENTON: Oh, I see. And how have you been keeping?

CONNIE: Oh, wonderfully well. I'm quite a different person since my operation.

FENTON: (*Smiling*) Good.

162

(*FENTON makes himself comfortable; pulls the safety belt round his jacket*)

CONNIE: (*Smiling at him*) Well, this is nice. I love company when I'm travelling, don't you?

(*The STEWARDESS passes down the corridor*)

FENTON: (*Flattering her*) It depends on the company.

CONNIE: (*Pleased*) Oh …

FENTON: I think you'd better fasten your safety belt.

(*CONNIE does*)

CONNIE: (*Gaily*) You know, I'm terrified of flying.

FENTON: Nonsense, I'll bet you love every minute of it.

CONNIE: I don't, honestly. I'm petrified. The funny thing is, I fly everywhere.

(*She smiles at FENTON; makes herself comfortable*)

CONNIE: Well, there's one thing, Mr Fenton. I shan't be able to tell you about my operation.

(*FENTON laughs*)

CUT TO: As before but now the ashtray on the table is full of cigarette ends; the magazines are open.

CONNIE is dozing. FENTON is reading a book. CONNIE opens her eyes.

CONNIE: Oh, dear, I've been asleep.

(*FENTON puts his book down on the table*)

CONNIE: What time is it?

FENTON: (*Looking at his watch*) Quarter past nine. We should be landing in about ten minutes.

(*CONNIE straightens her dress; takes out her lipstick and powder compact*)

CONNIE: I do wish we were staying longer in Cannes. Half an hour – it's absurd.

FENTON: What time do you get to Tunis?

163

CONNIE: Oh, don't! I think it's half past four or five or something. I shall look absolutely deadly. (*Using lipstick*) How long have I been asleep?

FENTON: About two hours.

(*CONNIE replaces the lipstick in her handbag which is on the table*)

CONNIE: Did I snore?

FENTON: Beautifully.

CONNIE: (*Suddenly; quite brightly*) Mr Fenton, I wonder if you'd be a darling and do me a favour?

FENTON: Yes, of course. What is it?

CONNIE: Well, I have a friend in Cannes – his name's Jerry Morgan, he's with the Trans-Rex Oil Company. He's flying to London tomorrow and he asked me to get him a seat for the first night of that new show – you know, the big American thing that's on at the er – what's it …

FENTON: (*Amused*) You mean …

CONNIE: You know – 'Kiss The Girls' or 'Chase Me Charley' or something!

FENTON: (*Laughing*) Yes, I know the one you mean.

CONNIE: (*Taking an envelope out of her handbag*) Well, I got him a seat all right, but like a silly ass I've brought the ticket with me.

FENTON: (*Quietly*) I see.

CONNIE: So, if you would be a darling and deliver it to him …?

(*She offers FENTON the envelope … After a momentary hesitation he takes it*)

FENTON: Er – yes, of course. Jerry Morgan, you said. Trans-Rex Oil Company.

CONNIE: Yes. (*Quite innocently; smiling at him*) You needn't worry about the customs. There's nothing

164

else in the envelope, I assure you. It's just a plain ordinary theatre ticket.

(*FENTON stares at her for a moment, then gives a nervous smile. The STEWARDESS arrives*)

STEWARDESS: Fasten your safety belts, please! (*To FENTON*) Fasten your safety belt, sir!

(*FENTON looks at the envelope in his hand, then up at the STEWARDESS*)

FENTON: Oh, dear!

STEWARDESS: What's the matter, sir?

FENTON: This is where I came in!

(*FENTON fastens his safety belt*)

THE END

My First Television Serial

By Francis Durbridge

Although I am known principally as the author of the Paul Temple stories, and although the new television serial will be Produced by Martyn C. Webster, *The Broken Horseshoe* is not a *Paul Temple* adventure. I should like to make that point quite clear because a great many people have already written to me wishing "Paul Temple" and "Steve" the best of luck with their television debut.

Mark Fenton, the principal character in *The Broken Horseshoe*, is quite different from Temple. To start with he is neither a novelist not a private detective – he doesn't even read detective stories! – and he is a bachelor. Whether he will stay that way remains to be seen.

The mystery starts when a man called Charles Constance is knocked down by a car, taken to one of the London hospitals, and operated on by Mark Fenton. A certain amount of the action of the first episode takes place in the hospital, but viewers need have no fear that there is undue emphasis on the less pleasant aspects of hospital life. It is essentially a mystery story, unfolded against a London background but with a particular interest for Midland viewers.

The part of Mark Fenton is played by John Robinson, whom viewers will remember in *The Night of the Fourth* and *The Cocktail Party*, and theatre-goers in the West-End production of *Edward, My Son*. With him is a strong team including John Byron, Andrew Crawford, Elizabeth Maude, Barbara Lott, and Robert Adair.

Although this is the first television serial I have written I have, like most writers, been interested in the medium since the early pre-war transmissions from Alexandra Palace. During a trip to the United States in 1949 I was fortunate enough to spend nearly a month popping in and out of the studios, watching rehearsals, and discussing the problems which face all writers and producers when – with trepidation – they turn towards the magic of television.

Martyn Webster and I have been working on *The Broken Horseshoe* for many weeks, but what you will see on your screens will not, by any means, be simply the product of my imagination and Webster's production. A television production, whether it is a play or a variety show, is the result of a great deal of hard work done by a great many people whose face you never see and whose names you never hear. I don't think this point can be too strongly emphasised.

Writing for television presents many difficulties, particularly for the writer who has specialised in sound radio. Every radio writer develops his own tricks for catching the listener's interest and holding it. In television he finds he has to discard some of these while others have to be reshaped to utilise the extra possibilities offered by a visual medium. However, speaking as a writer who has had a certain amount of experience with the writing of books and films as well as sound radio programmes, I think this business of television technique can, from a writer's point of view, be over-emphasised. In writing a show for television the main object is precisely the same as in writing a radio show, a stage play, or a film – namely to entertain. It is important not to lose sight of this fact.

I should like to recount a perfectly true story. When I landed in New York I had, like everyone else, to find a Customs official to check my baggage. Eventually I found one – a tall, tough, poker-faced individual. He went through my cases with a fine-tooth comb and eventually extracted a copy of one of my radio-thrillers. He turned it over, examined the cover, looked at the binding, flicked the pages – presumably in search of hidden diamonds. Eventually he looked up and opened the side of his mouth: "What's d'is?"

I said it was the script of a play.

"A moider player?" I said yes, it was a murder play.

He shook his head and raised his hand in a gesture of despair. "Every week I listen to d'ese things on the radio," he said. "An' every week they get worse an' worse!"

In a meek little voice I said: "That's why I'm here – this one gets better and better."

By Timothy, I hope you'll think that about *The Broken Horseshoe*.

Press Pack

Press cuttings about The Broken Horseshoe ...

Short Switch Not Sound Policy by Peter D. Cross

Can television programmes – which are so essentially visual in content – be produced by men who have been trained in radio for most of their lives?

The BBC policy is to "second" radio men to TV for short periods, in which time they are supposed to pick up all the tricks of the camera, learn about settings, and train their creative instincts to think in terms of Vision.

At the end of this time they are put in sole command of a TV show.

They do not have time even to learn from their mistakes, because a few weeks later they are back at their old jobs in radio – this time trying to think in terms of Sound.

It is a ridiculous policy, and the folly of it is emphasised when you check the numbers of TV producers who have really mastered the camera and Vision viewpoint.

Martyn C. Webster is a brilliant Sound producer – and he's been 25 years in radio. Now he has been attached to TV for six months.

On March 15 he will produce "*The Broken Horseshoe,*" a six-instalment mystery play by Francis Durbridge.

It will be interesting to see how much Vision technique Mr Webster can absorb by then.

Play Rehearsal by David R. Dewar

The first TV play to be seen in Scotland will be the opening instalment on Saturday night of the new serial, "*The Broken Horseshoe.*"

Judging from my impressions at a rehearsal this week this should be most successful in securing that essential response of an audience to the first part of the serial – impatience to know what happens next.

That was certainly my desire after I had watched producer Martyn Webster directing the cast on a run-through of the first episode.

The rehearsal took place, not in a studio, but in a reception hall in Marylebone, one of over a score of such halls used by the BBC for the preliminary "work outs" of TV plays. Only the final rehearsal takes place in the studio.

In the earlier stages the actors work from a plan of the studio. Mr Webster showed me the plan for this play, in which the scale is worked out to a quarter of an inch.

The designer has to use this plan when drawing the sets, and there has also to be conferences with the camera and lighting technicians.

Add to all this that various film shots have to taken and fitted in and you will have some idea of the complexity of a TV producer's job.

"We've finished the film scenes for this play," Mr Webster said. "They were shot at St Mary's Hospital, Paddington, and the authorities couldn't have been more helpful."

At a rehearsal interval I had a talk with the star, John Robinson, who will play the central figure in the serial, a London surgeon who becomes involved in a murder mystery.

Robinson is one of the finest actors in TV drama, and his recent roles include important parts in *"The Cocktail Party,"* *"The Night of the Fourth,"* and *"Dear Brutus."*

Robinson has not long returned from Australia, where he toured in a play with Elizabeth Bergner. His recipe for good TV acting could be summarised in the words, "Be subdued" and "Be sincere." "Any lack of sincerity is sure to be shown up by the TV cameras," he emphasised.

Another member of the cast is Glasgow actor Andrew Crawford who will be playing a Scottish doctor.

"I'm glad I won't need to bother about the right accent this time," he told me. "When I was playing in *"The Holly and the Ivy*" in the West End I had constantly to remember that I was supposed to be an Aberdonian.

"Luckily, most people in the audience in a London theatre don't know the difference."

He had a succinct summing-up of the test TV imposes on actors – "You either thrive on it or you die on it."

Saturday Serial by David R. Dewar

On the night of the 15th, if all goes well, Scottish viewers will be able to start a new TV serial at the beginning. The first instalment has been carefully timed with that object, and to avoid the frustration of new viewers "coming in at the middle."

Evening Times readers will have particular interest in the story to be televised as it is the work of Francis Durbridge creator of our "strip detective" Paul Temple.

Previously, Paul was one of radio's most popular characters, and his adventures were produced by Martyn C. Webster, who has now been seconded from sound to vision for six months and joins the impressive team of Scottish TV producers.

Webster's main assignment during these six months will be this new serial, and he gave me some advance information about it which encourages high expectations of its entertainment quality.

"This new Saturday serial will be a mystery thriller and will centre on the adventures of a London doctor," he told me. "One of the subsidiary characters will be a Scot, and I'm looking for an actor to take this part."

Martyn C. Webster has very definite views on TV drama, and is looking forward to this opportunity of carrying them into practice.

"I find this new medium a stimulating challenge," he said. "Sound producers have a great deal to learn before embarking on TV, and I find my stage experience very helpful.

173

"To my mind intimate drama with a few well-defined characters in homely and domestic settings is much more effective on television than ambitious and spectacular affairs. Too many people in the limited confines of a TV screen often lose all dramatic identity and become a confusing conglomeration to the spectator.

"The ideal television play is one in which the viewer is looking through a window into a room next door and observing what is going on within."

He had a few trenchant comments to make, this time in his private capacity as a Scottish viewer, on certain television tendencies which he claims should be corrected if Caledonian criticism is to be forestalled.

"Some of our features are becoming too Americanised, and there is a lavish and indiscriminate use of first names. A little more reticence and dignity (which doesn't mean pomposity) will go down better in Scotland."